JOHANN PETER HEBEL

THE TREASURE CHEST

STORIES, ILLUSTRATED WITH
CONTEMPORARY WOODCUTS

INTRODUCED AND TRANSLATED BY JOHN HIBBERD

PENGUIN BOOKS

PENGUIN BOOKS

Published by the Penguin Group
Penguin Books Ltd, 27 Wrights Lane, London W8 5TZ, England
Penguin Books USA Inc., 375 Hudson Street, New York, New York 10014, USA
Penguin Books Australia Ltd, Ringwood, Victoria, Australia
Penguin Books Canada Ltd, 10 Alcorn Avenue, Toronto, Ontario, Canada M4V 3B2
Penguin Books (NZ) Ltd, 182–190 Wairau Road, Auckland 10, New Zealand

Penguin Books Ltd, Registered Offices: Harmondsworth, Middlesex, England

Stories by J. P. Hebel mostly selected from *Schatzkästlein des
rheinischen Hausfreunde*, first published in 1811
This translation first published in Great Britain by Libris 1994
Published in Penguin Books 1995

5

The illustrations in this edition are mostly taken from *Der Rheinländische Hausfreund*,
where the stories were first published (courtesy Badische Landesbibliothek, Karlsruhe)

Printed in Great Britain by Clays Ltd, St Ives plc

www.greenpenguin.co.uk

Penguin Books is committed to a sustainable future
for our business, our readers and our planet.
The book in your hands is made from paper
certified by the Forest Stewardship Council.

Contents

The Treasure Chest

Introduction

Elias Canetti tells in his autobiography of his delight at discovering that Franz Kafka had called one famous piece from Hebel's *The Treasure Chest* ('Unexpected Reunion', p. 25) 'the most wonderful story in the world'. Canetti's own reaction to Hebel was thus confirmed by a fellow twentieth-century writer, and for him that was important. He knew that generations of ordinary Germans had loved Hebel's stories since their appearance in 1811. Yet the schoolmaster and cleric Hebel scarcely fitted modern notions of the literary genius. Might the common reader have been too easily pleased? Kafka and Canetti, and others with high demands of literature, thought not. They, like Goethe in Hebel's own time, recognized that Hebel's collection of tales lives up to its title: it contains real gems of imaginative fiction. Great discoveries await the English reader who comes across it for the first time.

This treasure trove is not unlike a child's box of treasures, and that is part of its charm. It inspires uncommon fondness. Some of its contents are unpretentious, consolation prizes, it might seem, in the treasure hunt Hebel invites us to enjoy; but they are presented with such charm that even the most sophisticated of readers may accept them too with a smile of pleasure. They grow in value with familiarity. The great prizes can, of course, be hunted systematically, by reading the collection through from beginning to end, even if in his original foreword the author himself, in characteristically teasing fashion, advised his readers that the best items might not be found at the beginning, but towards the middle or end of his volume. *The Treasure Chest* is, however, also there to be dipped into in the expectation of turning up something amusing or sad, curious, instructive or consoling, whatever suits a personal taste or a particular mood. It has something for almost everybody, things which invite repeated reading, prove unforgettable and give lasting enjoyment.

The sheer variety of the pieces and their brevity makes this book very unlike what the modern reader expects to find on the fiction shelves of the bookshop or library. Clearly the collection would be comparable to a Readers' Digest, were it not the creation of one person, bearing the unmistakable unifying stamp of his personality. Because it also has the marked and intriguing flavour of a particular time and place and because it is eminently suitable for the young and for reading aloud to others it might just be grouped with something like Uncle Remus's Brer Rabbit stories. Yet any such comparison is likely to be misleading. Hebel's delightful mixture of sentiment and humour is, for instance, similar to the quality which has made *A Christmas Carol* favourite reading down the ages. Yet his prose is unique. And unlike any Digest *The Treasure Chest* has become an enduring popular classic. Why was this? Who was the author Hebel, and how did he come to write the stories or articles, the anecdotes, vignettes, reports and jokes found in this volume? In answering these questions and attempting to explain the impact of his work, which some (paradoxically perhaps, given Hebel's down-to-earth attitudes) have understandably called quite magical, we shall see that Hebel the man and Hebel the writer were very much of one piece.

Johann Peter Hebel rose from very humble origins to become a schoolmaster and leading churchman; he knew the mind and the language of the ordinary people for whom he wrote the pieces he put into *The Treasure Chest*. His father (Johann Jakob Hebel, 1720–61) trained as a weaver before economic circumstances led him in 1747 to leave his native Palatinate in south-west Germany. Johann Jakob entered the service of a well-to-do citizen of Basel in Switzerland who as a major in the French army took him with him as batman on his campaigns. This batman was a cut above the ordinary: he filled two books with explanations of the principles and practical applications of arithmetic and kept notebooks in both German and French in which he recorded his journeys and copied out pages of poetry and prose, both pious and profane. It was in his master's house in Basel that he met Ursula Oertlin (1726–73), a peasant's daughter from the Wiese valley in the Black Forest in the margravate of Baden who was a maid in the same household. They were married in 1759 in a village in Baden. The ceremony could not be held in Basel, where mixed marriages were not allowed (he was of the Reformed Church, she a Lutheran). Their son was to be convinced, perhaps by the particular example provided by his parents as much as by the climate of enlightened thought in the eighteenth century, that love, common sense and humanity could and should transcend the barriers between different religions. The newly-weds lived in the tiny town of Hausen in the Black Forest that winter, where he worked as a weaver, and both returned to service with the Iselin family in Basel the next summer. (Hebel was later to write of men from small communities who could not support themselves all the year round from their craft or trade.) Johann Peter, born on 10 May 1760, was their first child. A year later his sister, Susanne, was born, but in the same year, 1761, she and their father died, victims of an epidemic in Basel. The widowed mother continued to live part of the year in Hausen, part in Basel, so the young Hebel received his earliest education in the country and in town and got to know the lives of peasants and burghers and the minds of rich and poor. He was thirteen years old and had begun to attend the grammar school in the town of Lörrach in the Black Forest when he learnt that his mother had fallen ill in Basel and had died on the road between there and Hausen. The vanity of earthly things, of which his pious mother must often have spoken, was an early and unforgettable part of his experience.

Ursula Hebel had wished for her son to enter the Lutheran Church. His teachers had reason to hope that he would be worthy of such a career, for he was a very promising pupil. With that future in mind, and with the help of money from the Iselin family and the proceeds of the sale of his mother's house in Hausen, the orphan was sent to the most prestigious school in Baden. Sporting his first pair of shoes he travelled for four days from the Wiese valley to the 'Gymnasium illustre' in the state capital Karlsruhe, and there over the next four years he maintained his early academic promise. In 1778 he went to study theology at university in Erlangen. By 1780 he had qualified for the ministry, but he was not offered a parish. It appears that he had somehow disappointed the teachers and clergymen who had high hopes of him. It can only be surmised that he had not been too assiduous in his theological studies and that his examination results were not outstanding. In Erlangen he could not afford orgies even if he had desired such indulgence, yet the signs are that he led a relaxed student's life. He had joined a duelling club, kept a dog as his constant companion, and was seldom seen without his pipe. His later writings suggest that he distinguished between religious faith and doctrinal pedantry, practical and theoretical Christianity. Neither that attitude nor the fact that he was never a killjoy and was always to appreciate convivial evenings at a hostelry need, however, have debarred him from a country living. But unknown to him in 1780 his dreams of a parish in the Black Forest were never to be realized.

The next ten years of his life were spent in relative poverty. He was a tutor to a rural vicar's children, then a teacher at a school in Lörrach, with its 1,700 inhabitants the largest town in the Wiese valley. Those years were in retrospect to appear the happiest of his life. He was in the countryside he loved best, read a great deal, and had the opportunity to explore the Black Forest and to travel into Switzerland and Alsace. His treatment of carefree wanderers in his later writings indicates that he cherished the chance to roam the countryside and be free of responsibilities. In Lörrach he found three lifelong friends in a fellow teacher, a young clergyman, and the teacher's sister-in-law. His relationship with her, Gustave Fecht, was a close one, but for long he was too poor to marry, and afterwards, for reasons which his biographers have failed to unearth, he never proposed to her. During this time in Lörrach he expressed the liberalness of his faith by indulging with a select group of friends in a fantastic semi-jocular cult of Proteus whom they revered as the spirit of the perpetual mutability of the world. He found release for his imagination in this cult and a temporary escape from philistinism in the tiny secret society of friends with its own secret language. He was able to sympathize with the polytheism that sees nature full of spirits. His Christianity was always to have a pantheistic tinge.

In 1791 Hebel, now thirty-one, moved back to his old school in Karlsruhe as a teacher. He was simultaneously appointed to the position of subdeacon, which meant he preached once a month before the Margrave and his court. That was not a task he relished, he would have preferred a congregation of farmers, but he was valued for the feeling and the wit he put into his sermons. He was appreciated as an outstanding teacher too. He prepared his lessons thoroughly and had a special gift for clear exposition. His subjects were Hebrew, Greek, Latin, and geography; he also taught mathematics and nature studies. In 1793 when French Revolutionary forces approached the capital of Baden he took over the duties of the distinguished teacher of botany and biology, Gmelin, when Gmelin left Karlsruhe together with the Margrave and his entourage who sought safety further east. Hebel protested his incompetence as a natural scientist, but within a few years he had been invited to join leading German scientific societies. In 1798 he was promoted, with the title of Professor of Theology and Hebrew. He was drawing a good salary. He was entrusted with important tasks within the Church: composing prayers for regular use in services and revising the catechism. Yet he yearned to return to the Black Forest region. Even after thirty years in Karlsruhe he was still to write to his best friend in Lörrach that he felt a foreigner in the town on the plain and was moved to tears when he set eyes on a young soldier from his native valleys.

It was five years before Hebel visited what he regarded as his home country. From Karlsruhe he had gone on botanizing trips with Gmelin, who was to name a plant family after him (in vain, for it had already been named by William Hudson). He had made two longish journeys in 1794 and 1795. But not until the autumn of 1796 did he go back to the Black Forest and Basel. On this holiday trip he witnessed the French under General Moreau retreating over the Rhine and the effects of war on the civilian population who suffered from the requisitioning and looting by both sides. The cannon were still ringing in his ears when he arrived back in Karlsruhe. (No wonder that so many of his stories, written during or just after the exploits of Napoleon, tell of such times of war.) In the spring of 1799 and the autumn of 1801 he went 'home' again. It was in the months before and after the visit in 1801 that he wrote his *Alemannische Gedichte*, the most famous volume of dialect poetry in German.

He had become interested in medieval German, the history of the language and the place of Alemannic in that development. He hoped to persuade others that the dialect of his native region was not a deformed version of standard modern German but a language with great merits of its own and a distinguished pedigree. According to contemporary experts it shared the name Alemannic with the language of the great medieval poets, the Minnesänger. His stated aim in the *Alemannische Gedichte* was to ennoble the language he had spoken before coming to Karlsruhe, to put it to edifying purpose and reveal its inherent 'poetry'. But his real inspiration was simply his nostalgic love for his favourite countryside and its inhabitants. His loving imagination transfigured the landscape and the people. In these poems he anthropomorphizes the whole of nature. The river Wiese becomes a Black Forest girl who falls into the arms of the handsome Rhine. He invents his own mythology, drawing on local superstition and on the make-believe world of his earlier cult of Protean nature. He writes as if with the mind of the region's peasant inhabitants. Few of them could have read these poems when they were published in 1803. But in the course of time they became as familiar to them as the Bible and their own folksongs, and nowadays the name Hebel is as meaningful to the people of the south-west corner of Germany, Alsace and Switzerland, where Alemannic is spoken, as Robbie Burns is to the Scots. And very soon he had a public among educated Alemannic speakers, and among Germans from other areas too, for whom he provided brief notes on vocabulary, grammar and pronunciation. The volume was greeted enthusiastically by leading writers of the time, including Goethe. Jean Paul, an author whom Hebel greatly admired, declared that one could never tire of reading these poems over and over again. Contemporaries were impressed by the charm of poetry that breathed the spirit of a particular countryside; it seemed above all natural.

The dialect gave Hebel's verses a unique vigour and freshness. Nevertheless he did not draw simply on folk tradition. The *Alemannische Gedichte* contain simple folksong-like strophes, but also more meditative and narrative pieces in blank verse and astonishingly convincing classical hexameters. Hebel transports his reader into the Wiese valley and the real details of its topography, not into a stylized Arcadia, and escapes the conventions of idyllic verse. Yet the influence of one of his favourite poets, Theocritus, can still be felt as a major presence. Besides, he had no desire to deny the spirit of his age and his calling as pedagogue and clergyman. He wished to improve his readers, to nourish their feeling for nature, their moral sense and their religious faith. He fitted ghosts and will-o'-the-wisps into an optimistic Christian framework. One of his poems, 'Der Statthalter von Schopfheim', transfers the story of David, Nabal and Abigail into the Black Forest setting. Because his convictions were so secure he was never aggressively didactic. He could range easily from nature poetry to songs and dialogues and a frightening ballad, and allow himself a playful tone and a sense of humour. The dialect medium lent itself to the inclusion of proverbial and down-to-earth pieces of wisdom. Hebel knew that its speakers did not indulge in pathos. But the strength of his religious faith is expressed in one of the greatest poems on mortality in any language, 'Die Vergänglichkeit' (rendered as 'Sic transit' in Leonard Forster's *Penguin Book of German Verse*). Here Hebel draws on memories of his mother's death on the road to Hausen. In the poem a father tells his young son in simple and sober words that all things must pass, the whole world, even the familiar mountains, the river Wiese, the city of Basel and its seemingly permanent church of St Peter will one day be destroyed: all men must age and die, but those who act as conscience dictates will rise from the dead and be taken to the happier homeland up above. This moving piece has found a secure place in anthologies of German poetry.

Hebel did not think of himself as a poetic genius. Early on he realized that the verses he wrote as a child inspired by the German poets of the mid-eighteenth century were of no value. At the age of twenty-eight, on reading the Minnesänger, he had tried his hand at verses in Alemannic, but without success. His lack of poetic gifts seemed to be certain. Thirteen years later, however, inspiration had come, and with it general acclaim. The first, anonymous, edition of the *Alemannische Gedichte* was printed on a subscription basis and Hebel's best friend from his time in Lörrach did valiant work collecting advance orders. Within a year, however, a second edition had appeared above the author's name. Two more were published by 1808. Yet Hebel was not persuaded that inspiration would ever come again. For the fifth edition (1820) he was able to add a few more poems to the thirty-two from 1803. But he wrote philosophically, 'The Muse is not always with me, she only visits me' and that there was nothing to be gained from forcing her against her will.

In 1806 the long-awaited opportunity to return to the Black Forest region offered itself. The largely Catholic Breisgau was – as one consequence of the battle of Austerlitz – incorporated into Baden and the town of Freiburg was to be provided with a Lutheran pastor. Hebel was offered the position. But he hesitated, and bowed to the wish of his ruler (now, thanks to Napoleon, a Grand Duke) that he should remain in Karlsruhe. For he was a valued member of the Lutheran establishment in the capital and at court. Soon, in 1808, he became headmaster of his school, where his main worries were that the classrooms were simply not big enough to accommodate the pupils (one of the classes numbered eighty-three boys). He remained in that post until 1814. After that he continued to teach at the same school, but as he rose to the top of the Lutheran hierarchy in Baden his energies were increasingly concentrated on Church matters. From 1803 to 1814, however, the school establishment and the state required his services as editor and author.

It was not inspiration but duty which moved Hebel to write the prose pieces which became as famous as the *Alemannische Gedichte* when put together in the *Treasure Chest* (the *Schatzkästlein des rheinischen Hausfreundes*, 1811). They were provided to order, but written according to his own plan, in his spare time and with commitment and pleasure too.

The ruler of Baden from 1746 till 1811, Karl Friedrich, was a typical enlightened prince of the times. He was one of the first in Germany to abolish serfdom (in 1783) and to emancipate the Jews (in 1809). (Hebel's attitude towards monarchy was determined by the relatively happy circumstances in the small state of Baden as well as by his Lutheranism and his loyalty to a system in which he made his own career.) One of Karl Friedrich's concerns was education, which he saw as a key to economic advance and the improvement of his subjects. The grammar school in Karlsruhe was close to his heart, and since 1750 it had been entrusted with the preparation of all books for use in churches and schools in the margravate and with the compilation and sale of the Lutheran almanac for Baden. The school had leased the rights over the almanac to publishers, but they lost money and the school was obliged to reassume responsibility for a publication which had been meant to bring the institution revenue but instead had become a financial burden. The problem was not solved when the government ruled that every household was obliged to buy a copy, since that only made for greater consumer resistance. The product was simply not as good as some of its competitors from other states. In 1802 Hebel was one of five wise men who discussed the situation, but as he put it, 'many cooks spoil the broth', and sales of the *Curfürstlich badischer gnädigst privilegirter Landkalender für die badische Margravschaft lutherischen Antheils* fell further. In 1806 Hebel made suggestions of his own. The almanac should be given a snappier and more attractive name: the Landkalender's longwinded and clumsy title served only to warn the public: 'Don't buy me, I'm not for you!' The technical presentation had to be improved and the publication must be put in the hands of one man, someone close to the majority of the people, the rural population, for whom the almanac was intended.

Hebel had a friend of his, a country clergyman, in mind, but inevitably he was charged with carrying out his own proposals for reform. So the almanacs for 1808 to 1811, now named *Der Rheinländische Hausfreund*, were the work of Hebel alone. He was also solely responsible for the issues for the years from 1812 to 1815, and again for the 1819 edition. Already by 1810 Goethe, having seen one issue which he found delightful, was anxious to lay hands on more. Individual items from the *Hausfreund* were reprinted in major German periodicals. They had proved to be of more than local relevance and interest. The almanac began to sell outside Baden. And the leading publisher Cotta asked Hebel to put together a selection intended not just for the publication of Baden but for the wider German public. It appeared as *The Treasure Chest – Schatzkästlein des rheinischen Hausfreundes –*

containing one hundred and twenty-eight pieces from the years 1803 to 1811.

The almanac was usually the only reading matter in the ordinary household apart from the Bible and the Hymn or Prayer Book and was therefore seen as an important means of improving the people. It contained by definition the calendar for the year. By tradition it also brought instructive and improving items. Hebel had been writing pieces for it since 1803. Before 1808 his contributions had taken two main forms. He wrote instructive articles on natural history: on the processional caterpillars to be found in native oak woods; on the miracle of natural propagation by seed; on snakes, spiders and moles. The item on moles has been included in the present volume; it shows his gift as a teacher who calls on his pupils to recognize the value of expert knowledge and to act upon it. It also reveals him in what we would now call a green role. Elsewhere too he dwells on the wonders of nature and the wisdom of God's creation. He pours scorn on superstition and fantastic myth, but exotic and incredible things are related as bait for the reader. There are fish that fly! Stories about the tarantula are to be regarded with caution, some spiders are poisonous, but not those in Germany; only the credulous believe in dragons! He warns strongly against the fashion for tight garters worn by men below the knee, they restrict the circulation which works like an irrigation system in the fields – and what happens to plants that are deprived of water? After 1807 more similarly practical advice was to follow, on the preparation of corn seed, how to make ink, to preserve wooden posts from rot or to care for fruit trees, or why clothing should be disinfected after illness. Each issue brought descriptions of the heavenly bodies and the laws which regulate their movements, all in the language the common man could follow. But already, before he was responsible for the almanac, Hebel contributed little amusing or intriguing anecdotes with an explicit or implied moral. The moral might simply involve a suggestion for the treatment of arrogance and testiness, as in 'Dinner Outside' (p. 7) and 'The Clever Judge' (p. 8), two pieces from 1803.

As sole contributor Hebel increased the number and variety of narrative items and set the reader riddles to solve. His material was seldom if ever original. 'A Strange Walk and Ride' (p. 23), for instance, is a version of a parable that has been told many times and is perhaps best known from the Fables of La Fontaine. Hebel drew on anything he read, heard or overheard, and most of all on a collection of jokes and stories published in ten volumes from 1763 to 1792 (*Vade Mecum für lustige Leute* edited by Friedrich Nicolai). He had a genius for reducing a story to its essentials. But he spent much time and effort in rewriting the items. He hoped that this would not be noticed in the finished product which had to appear natural and spontaneous. Privately, however, he wrote of the pains he took: the articles might seem to be effortlessly natural, yet writing pieces which showed no sign of art or effort was more demanding than composing something more obviously impressive. He had two guides. One was the training in stylistics derived from his classical education. ('Kannitverstan' [p. 40], one of his most famous stories, started as a school exercise in Latin composition.) The other was his knowledge of the everyday language of ordinary people and his ear for the rhythms of their speech. For his aim as educator was to speak to the ordinary man in his own language. The task was made easier because he loved that language himself. Here, however, he made sparing use of dialect (and removed its most obvious features when revising his articles for inclusion in the *Schatzkästlein*). Yet the simple syntax, the pithy phrases, the freedom of word order, the avoidance of abstractions in favour of concrete analogies, in short the oral tone he adopted, has persuaded generations of readers that his work is natural, unstrained, and of the people. The impression of unsophisticated oral narration was strengthened by the rarity of paragraph divisions, though that may also have been determined by the need to save paper (some improvements to the almanac that he desired proved too expensive). His punctuation was (by the standards of later German) unorthodox: his commas usually indicate pauses rather than boundaries between grammatical clauses as would be required by normal German usage, and even his full stops can seem strangely placed, marking sometimes a break as soon as a new idea is to be taken up rather than before it is introduced. His prose, it has been said, must be read with the ear, not the eye. The repetitions, the variation of tense and the change of syntactical structure within a sentence are never overdone, but they too contribute to the impression that this is spontaneous oral narrative. Not all of these features have been consistently or precisely rendered in the translation. Use of the present tense in narrative, for instance, is not uncommon in spoken English, more especially among the uneducated, but in print nowadays it looks precious. And whereas traces of dialect are a normal feature of the German spoken by most social classes, in English dialect can too easily smack overmuch of quaintness. So something of Hebel's sophisticated unsophisticatedness has to be lost in translation. But perhaps not too much. For it would need great changes indeed to alter the basic flavour of Hebel's texts.

Much of that flavour derives from the presence of the author himself in his persona as the 'Hausfreund' (Family Friend). In the engraving on the title page of each almanac he stands in the centre of the picture, with the village church in the background, speaking to a dozen men and women carrying a scythe or a rake or a whip, one, the magistrate perhaps, in frock coat and knee breeches, a book in his hand. A child and a dog are listening too. This friend of the family gives good advice. He wishes others to share and benefit from his knowledge. But he also jokes and entertains. As he tells a story he anticipates questions from the audience, guesses their thoughts and keeps them guessing. Ignorant of the rules of nineteenth-century literary realism, he declares that the tale must proceed as he dictates. But Hebel had observed that the man in the street, or in the fields, did not want a diet of fairy-tales. So he gives date and place when reporting events from history, or establishes the location, as if he were telling of events that really happened, for items that are fictional. Occasionally he claims to have been present at the incident he relates – as in 'The Fake Gem' (p. 97) which, he says, took place in Strassburg where Hebel did in fact have good friends. He offers comments as he goes along (sometimes as Biblical quotations which he could expect his audience to recognize). He points out the moral in a brief prologue or, more often, in an epilogue accompanied by a wag of the finger – and sometimes a wink – and the catchword 'Merke!' ('Note this' or 'Remember!'). His readers, he knew, were practical people who wanted something with a message, but they also had minds of their own and were keen to use them – so sometimes they were left to work out the moral for themselves. The Hausfreund confesses why a certain story moves him, but puts the more gushing speeches on the marvellous beneficence of nature and God's creation in the mouth of his right-hand man or assistant ('der Adjunkt', a friend in Karlsruhe – the 'mother-in-law' who also appears was Henriette Hendel, an actress to whom the bachelor Hebel lost his heart in 1808). He addresses the reader as reader, not listener, but this does not necessarily destroy the illusion that oral communication is involved. The modern reader must therefore be aware that he has to adopt the right tone and to pace the story right if he is to satisfy himself as 'listener'. In many cases the reader of the *Hausfreund* in Hebel's time would be reading aloud to family or friends. The fact that he was then standing in for the Family Friend could give a special twist to Hebel's phrase 'der geneigte Leser versteht's' (the good or kind reader will understand). But in any case the narrator can always assume that his readers or listeners are no fools and that he has not spoken above their heads. They are assumed to be his equals in faith, intelligence and common sense if not in knowledge, and he can establish a relationship of intimacy with them. The Hausfreund puts us at our ease, much as a BBC radio programme for young listeners used to with its opening words, 'Are you sitting comfortably? Then we'll begin!' His good humoured and reassuring presence is felt even in those narrative items where he keeps his distance.

Sales of the almanac increased dramatically as soon as Hebel had taken over. Clearly he knew how to speak to the common reader. His persona as Family Friend was part of a successful formula. Other almanacs posed as the work of one 'Calendar Man' – it was not a new trick, but in this case it worked better. For Hebel could become the Family Friend with no difficulty at all; he was to a large extent being himself, talking to his fellow countrymen who did not all have the advantage of his education and access to books. But Hebel's secret to success was that he knew what the readers wanted. Many of them had difficulty reading, many would have to be read to, so the items had to be short. They must also be varied.

Hebel aimed to satisfy different tastes by including comic anecdotes, stories of executions and murders, reports of sensations, disasters and mysteries. He included jokes too, and childish or silly some of them may seem, but they serve to establish that the Hausfreund is no snobbishly superior being, he can enjoy simple jokes like anyone else. A young woman of whom Hebel was fond, mother to some of his several godchildren, was astounded and embarrassed that he did not stand on his dignity with her. She was, she said later, too naïve herself to appreciate naturalness. She would have preferred to find a hero in him. But Hebel himself liked to put inhibitions aside when with friends, and it was as a friend that he spoke to his readers.

Of all the comic pieces, those involving a trio of likeable rogues have proved enduringly popular. Here the author makes no pretence at improving the reader and shares the peasant's (and not only the peasant's) typical delight in the triumph of cunning and ingenuity. With him we can admire the pranks of 'der Zundelfrieder' (Freddy Tinder) and his companions in eight stories, sympathize with these characters' pride in their skill and quickwittedness, and share their love of adventure, almost forgetting that they are petty criminals. Individuals who use their heads are sure of Hebel's approbation. Other, equally entertaining pieces tell of how minor rogues are defeated by quick thinking and a sense of fun. Among the quite different items which cater for a taste for the sensational, reports of natural disasters could be used to suggest the need to be prepared for death or to be thankful if one was spared. Gruesome executions, often related with grim humour, lent themselves to illustrating the wages of sin. But not all such pieces have a moral. The appeal of 'A Secret Beheading' (p. 85) is in large part, as Hebel indicates at the end, that it combines sensation and mystery. When it comes to ghosts, on the other hand, he supposes rational explanations for their appearance – while still assuring us that in any case anyone with an easy conscience, like the hero of 'Settling Accounts with a Ghost' (p. 18), has no cause to fear spooks! But the rational explanation is given only after the thrill of fear has been exploited, just as elsewhere the reader is likely to experience a shudder of revulsion at cruelty and murder before the story shows that murder does not pay.

Hebel does not play down the harshness of existence, least of all the horrors of war. He condemns cruelty and senseless destruction, but more often he likes to tell how humanity can relieve suffering and how kindness or Christian virtue can be shown by anyone, by emperors and peasants alike. The great who exercise clemency or gratitude and are fair and just are not presented as faultless heroes, they are simply behaving as good men; their acts are all the more exemplary because they are done by individuals with common human failings. Very ordinary men and women too can perform what are almost miracles of kindness and justice. They do not need to be Lutheran or even Christian. That God operates through the most unlikely of men and women is cause for marvel and heartfelt gratitude. Thus tolerance is one of the great virtues espoused by the Hausfreund and set against arrogance and bigotry. It is extended most noticeably to the Jews. Hebel bases stories on their wiliness and love of profit, but he suggests that those characteristics are not in themselves despicable and that Jews would be no different from everyone else if they were treated fairly and accorded equality as citizens and fellow human beings.

Hebel's sympathy with the little man might suggest revolutionary leanings. But his political stance is best described as cautiously liberal. He intimates that in a revolution the most unsuitable persons may be appointed to positions of authority ('A Willing Justice', p. 150), deplores acts of disloyalty or betrayal, and reports with approval how Napoleon restored law and order to revolutionary France. Like many German liberals at the time, he saw Napoleon not as a warmonger and tyrant but as the bringer of political and social reform. He illustrates the foolishness of rebelling against the given system of authority. Thus Andreas Hofer, celebrated in the Austrian Tyrol as a national hero, is presented in the *Schatzkästlein* (p. 122) as an obstinate fool who causes unnecessary suffering. In Hebel's age it was not unnatural to appreciate the value of political stability and to question the wisdom of the mob. His intended audience, citizens of a small state, were involved, as soldiers, victims or onlookers, and with various degrees of enthusiasm or reluctance, in events beyond their control. We do not need to be familiar with the details of each stage of the Napoleonic Wars, or to know, for instance, why Germans became allied with the French, in order to identify with this sense of powerlessness, and to appreciate the need felt in such times to hold fast to basic human values and find security in simple religious faith.

It will be clear that Hebel did not deal with narrowly local matters. The ordinary reader, he wrote, is curious, he wants to hear about things outside his own experience, about events beyond his village, town or state. So he tells of recent historical events and of curious or extraordinary happenings far away from the confines of Baden. He knew that great changes in contemporary Europe could threaten not just political but also moral and religious stability, and so often his stories show that good and admirable qualities remain good and admirable in any circumstances. For all his fascination with man's weaknesses and quirks Hebel was convinced that there was such a thing as human dignity, an enduring value which could be reconciled with tolerance and good humour.

The publisher of the *Schatzkästlein*, which went into a second edition in 1818, urged Hebel to prepare another volume of pieces from the *Hausfreund* after 1811, but in vain. It seems that Hebel was worried that such, often frivolous, things hardly befitted a man of his standing in the church establishment. (Not everyone needed to know that he kept an owl and a tree frog as pets.) The almanac for 1815 had caused him some unpleasantness. One anecdote in it, 'Pious Advice' (p. 150), was deemed offensive by the Catholic Church – reacting, perhaps, to attempts (which Hebel deplored) by the agents of the Lutheran almanac to force it upon Catholic households – and the whole almanac for that year had to be reprinted. Hebel's involvement in the *Hausfreund* after that would have been minimal but for the fact that a plan to contribute to another calendar fell through, so that the pieces he wrote for that separate venture could make up the volume for 1819. His great concern now was that the churches should work together for the benefit of the people. When in 1818 he was made Prelate of the Lutheran Church in Baden and thus became a member of the Diet in Karlsruhe (this parliament was one of the progressive results of the Napoleonic upheavals) he was concerned mainly with welfare measures to help widows and orphans, the blind and the deaf and dumb, and in this he worked closely with his Catholic counterpart. He also supported moves to liberalize the censorship of publications. His main preoccupation, however, was to bring the two Protestant Churches in Baden closer to each other.

In 1818 he began his Bible stories for children (*Biblische Geschichten*). They were intended to be used in both Lutheran and Reformed schools, which indeed they were, after their publication in 1824, until 1855. (There were moves in the Catholic hierarchy, much to Hebel's gratification, to place them in Catholic schools too.) Baden as Grand Duchy included large areas of population in the Reformed Palatinate, and thanks largely to Hebel's endeavours the Lutheran and Reformed Churches in Baden were united in 1821. He wrote parts of the liturgy which was used for more than thirty years. For this contribution to church history he was awarded an honorary doctorate in theology by the University of Heidelberg. It was while travelling between Mannheim and Heidelberg to examine students of theology that he died, of cancer it seems, in September 1826. In 1824 he had lost a great part of his wealth when his banker, a friend of his, went bankrupt. Characteristically the loss had been borne philosophically; Hebel was more concerned with the plight of his friend than with his own misfortune.

Each year on Hebel's birthday a ceremony, organized by the Hebel Foundation of Basel, takes place in his honour in his native Hausen. There are speeches, prizes for the young who recite his poems, gifts for virtuous fiancés or newly-weds, and a meal at which the oldest parishioners are the guests of honour. The celebration recalls a man whose work endeared itself to the local community and acted as its cultural ambassador. His fame went far. Tolstoy was able to recite some of Hebel's stories by heart. In translation they were popular with teachers and pupils alike in Russian schools. Their continuing appeal to adults throughout Germany (who fall in love with Freddy Tinder, the Sly Pilgrim [p. 31] and 'Kannitverstan' at an early age) is attested by the appearance every few years of a new inexpensive edition of his works. Such popularity and Hebel's early adoption as a text for schoolchildren seem, however, to have discouraged searching literary analysis of his work. Between the two world wars the influential critical rebel Walter Benjamin could accuse the literary establishment of having ignored Hebel's achievement by declaring his jewels of prose fit only for peasants and children. (Benjamin's friend Bertolt Brecht was to emulate, in his *Kalendergeschichten* [*Tales from the Calendar*] of 1948, Hebel's special art of using a brief story to make a particular point to a particular public.) Yet in fact Hebel never lacked fervent admirers among intellectuals. The philosopher Martin Heidegger, for instance, had an almost religious respect for Hebel, and though his approach may not convince everyone, there can be no doubt that he was reacting to something essential in Hebel's work, not only to his models of the art of prose narrative but to what earlier generations had been content to call naturalness. It was undoubtedly that secure naturalness that appealed so strongly to Kafka as a contrast to his own abysses of uncertainty. Hebel had no problems deciding what was true and what was right, when it was appropriate to laugh and when to cry, and the modern reader may well, like Kafka, find welcome relief from some of the products of modernism (and its successors) in an author who is eminently accessible, is not ashamed of sentiment, is cheerful and humorous and sane and humane.

The present edition brings, in translation, a selection from the *Schatzkästlein* of 1811, several pieces from later issues of the *Hausfreund*, one story ('Mr Charles', p. 161) that Hebel published elsewhere, and one ('The Glove Merchant', p. 166) which was first printed after his death. As translator I am grateful to Celia Skrine, who kindly looked through an early draft of many of the items in this volume, made suggestions for improvements and, equally important, gave encouragement. My thanks also to my publisher who retained his enthusiasm for the project throughout. He and I present this volume to the English-speaking world as Kafka presented his copy of the *Schatzkästlein* to an acquaintance, 'um Hebel eine Freude zu machen', but trusting that it will give pleasure to its readers too.

Further Reading

The literature on Hebel in English is sparse and to be found in academic periodicals. Two general essays suitable for the reader without German, but likely to be found only in university libraries, are: C. P. Magill, 'Pure and Applied Art: A Note on J. P. Hebel' in *German Life and Letters*, new series 10 (1956–57), pp. 183–188; J. Hibberd, 'J. P. Hebel' in *Dictionary of Literary Biography*, vol. 90, edited by J. Hardin and C. Schweitzer (Detroit, 1989), pp. 128–132.

The most accessible books in German are: U. Däster, *J. P. Hebel in Selbstzeugnissen und Bilddokumenten* (Reinbek, 1973) and R. M. Kully, *Johann Peter Hebel* (Stuttgart, 1969); W. Zentner, *J. P. Hebel* (Karlsruhe, 1965), is a fuller biography. L. Rohner, *Kalendergeschichte und Kalender* (Wiesbaden, 1978), places Hebel's stories within the history of German almanacs. Ambitious readers may also wish to consult Walter Benjamin, 'Zu J. P. Hebels 100. Geburtstag' in Benjamin, *Gesammelte Schriften II* (Frankfurt am Main, 1955, reprinted 1977) and Martin Heidegger, 'Sprache und Heimat' in *Über Johann Peter Hebel* (Tübingen, 1964 – tributes and essays by Heidegger, Theodor Heuss, Carl J. Burckhardt, Werner Bergengruen and others).

The original *Hausfreund* has been reproduced in facsimile as Hebel, *Der Rheinische Hausfreund, Faksimiledruck der Jahrgänge 1808–15 und 1819*, edited by L. Rohner (Wiesbaden, 1981). Hebel's *Schatzkästlein* is available in a convenient paperback with annotations by W. Theiss (Stuttgart, 1981, later reprints). Volumes 2 and 3 of Hebel's *Sämtliche Schriften*, edited by A. Braunbehrens *et al* (Karlsruhe, 1990) contain all his stories.

A Note on Currency

Gold doubloons and louis d'or should cause readers no problem. But they may wish to note that two silver coins, the thaler and the gulden (rendered as guilder), were in use in Baden and other German states in Hebel's time. They may be thought of as British crowns and halfcrowns, though they were worth rather less and varied in value according to where they were minted. Hebel sometimes called thalers silver crowns, and used the abbreviation fl (florin) for gulden. There were sixty kreuzers to a gulden. The name kreuzer has usually been retained in the translation, but for coins representing fractions or multiples of the kreuzer it sometimes seemed more natural to speak of pennies and farthings. Hebel himself assisted his German readers by occasionally switching from a foreign currency, e.g. French livres or francs, into thalers.

The Treasure Chest

What a Strange Creature is Man

A King of France was told by his valet about a man who was seventy-five years of age and had never been outside Paris: he had only heard talk of country lanes, the fields or springtime. You could tell him the world outside had come to an end twenty years ago, he'd have to believe you. The King asked if this man was ill or feeble. 'No,' said the valet, 'he's as healthy as a fish in water.' Did he suffer from melancholy? 'No, he's as happy as a sandboy.' Did he have to work to support a large family? 'No, he's well-to-do. He simply doesn't want to see anything else. He's not curious.' The King was intrigued and desired to see this man.

A King of France's desire is soon fulfilled, not every one of them of course, but this one was, and the King talked with the man about this and that and asked if he had always been happy and well. 'Yes, Sire,' he replied, 'all my seventy-five years.' Was he born in Paris? 'Yes, Sire! I could scarcely have got in any other way, for I've never been out.' 'That surprises me,' replied the King. 'That's why I had you summoned. I hear that you are in the habit of taking suspicious walks to one or other of the city gates! Do you know you have been watched for some time?' The man was astonished by this accusation and said it couldn't be him, someone of the same name perhaps or something like that. But the King cut him short: 'Not another word! I trust that in future you will not leave town again without my express permission!'

A real Parisian ordered to do something by the King doesn't spend long wondering if it's necessary or whether there isn't a better way of going about things, he does as he's told. Our man was a real Parisian, though when the mail coach passed him on his way home he thought, 'You lucky people in there, you can leave Paris!' Once home he read the paper as he did every day. But this time he didn't find much in it. He looked out of the window, but for once there was nothing of interest there. He started to read a book, but suddenly that seemed so pointless. He went for a walk, he went to the theatre, to the inn, but now it was all so dull. So the first quarter of the year passed, and the second, and more than once he said to those sitting next to him in the inn, 'My friends, it's a hard verdict, seventy-five years in Paris without a break, and now I am told I'm not allowed to leave town.'

Eventually in the third quarter he couldn't bear it any longer, and day after day he requested permission, the weather being so glorious, or nice and fresh from the rain. He would gladly pay for a trusty man to escort him, two if necessary. But it was no good. When however one painful year to the day had passed, and he came home that evening and asked his wife with a frown, 'What's that new carriage doing outside? Is someone making fun of me?' she replied, 'My dear, we've been looking for you everywhere! The King has given you the coach and permission to drive in it wherever you like.' 'Ma foi!' the man answered, and his face had relaxed, 'The King is just!' 'But what do you say,' his wife continued, 'why don't we go for a drive in the country tomorrow?' 'Well now,' said the man, and he showed no emotion, 'we'll see! If not tomorrow, perhaps another day. And anyway what would we do out there? Paris is nicest from the inside.'

The Silver Spoon

An officer in Vienna was thinking, 'Just for once I'll dine at the Red Ox,' and into the Red Ox he went. There were regulars there and strangers, important and unimportant people, honest men and rascals such as you'll find anywhere. They were eating and drinking, some a great deal, others little. They talked and argued about this and that, about how it had rained rocks at Stannern in Moravia, for instance, or about Machin who fought the great wolf in France.* When the meal was almost over one or two were drinking a small jug of Tokay to round things off, one man was making little balls from bread crumbs as if he were an apothecary making pills, another was fiddling with his knife or his fork or his silver spoon. It was then the officer happened to notice how a fellow in a green huntsman's coat was playing with a silver spoon when it suddenly disappeared up his sleeve and stayed there.

Someone else might have thought, 'It's no business of mine,' and said nothing, or have made a great fuss. The officer thought, 'I don't know who this green spoon-hunter is and what I might let myself in for,' and he kept as quiet as a mouse, until the landlord came to collect his money. But when the landlord came to collect his money the officer, too, picked up a silver spoon, and tucked it through two button holes in his coat, in one and out the other as soldiers sometimes do in war when they take their spoons with them, but no soup. As the officer was paying his bill the landlord was looking at his coat and thinking, 'That's a funny medal this gentleman's wearing! He must have distinguished himself battling with a bowl of crayfish soup to have got a silver spoon as a medal! Or could it just be one of mine?' But when the officer had paid the landlord he said, without a sign of a smile on his face, 'The spoon's included, I take it? The bill seems enough to cover it.' The landlord said, 'Nobody's tried that one on me before! If you don't have a spoon at home I'll give you a tin one, but you can't have one of my silver spoons!' Then the officer stood up, slapped the landlord on the shoulder and laughed. 'It was only a

* See Notes on pp. 173–5.

joke we were having,' he said, 'that gentleman over there in the green jacket and me! – My green friend, if you give back that spoon you have up your sleeve I'll give mine back too.' When the spoon-hunter saw that he had been caught in the act and that an honest eye had observed his dishonest hand, he thought, 'Better pretend it was a joke,' and gave back his spoon. So the landlord got his property back, and the spoon thief smiled too – but not for long. For when the other customers saw what had happened they set about him with curses and hounded him out of the Holy of Holies and the landlord sent the boots after him with a big stick. But he stood the worthy officer a bottle of Tokay to toast the health of all honest men.

Remember: You must not steal silver spoons!

Remember: Someone will always stand up for what is right.

The Cheap Meal

There is an old saying: The biter is sometimes bit. But the landlord at the Lion in a certain little town was bitten first. He received a well-dressed customer who curtly demanded a good bowl of broth, the best his money would buy. Then he ordered beef and vegetables too for his money. The landlord asked him, all politeness, if he wouldn't like a glass of wine with it. 'Indeed I would,' his guest replied, 'if I can have a good one for my money.' When he had finished, and he enjoyed it all, he took a worn six-kreuzer piece from his pocket and said, 'Here you are, landlord, there's my money!' The landlord said, 'What's this? You owe me a thaler!' The customer answered, 'I didn't ask for a meal for a thaler, but for my money. Here it is. It's all I have. If you gave me too much for it then that's your fault!' It wasn't really such a clever trick. It called only for cheek and a devil-may-care view of the consequences. But the best is yet to come.

'You're an utter villain,' said the landlord, 'and don't deserve this. But you can have the meal for nothing and take this twenty-four kreuzer bit as well. Just keep quiet about it and go over to my neighbour who keeps the Bear and try the same trick on him!' He said this because he had had a quarrel with his neighbour and resented his success and each was keen to do the other down.

But the artful customer smiled as he took the money he was offered in his one hand and reached carefully for the door with the other, wished the innkeeper good afternoon, and said, 'I went to the Bear first, it was the landlord there who sent me over here!'

So really both of the innkeepers had been tricked; the cunning customer took advantage of their quarrel. Yet he might have also earned a further reward, grateful thanks from both of them, if they had learnt the right lesson from it and had made things up between them. For peace pays, whereas quarrels have to be paid for.

Dinner Outside

We often complain how difficult or impossible it is to get on with certain people. That may of course be true. But many such people are not bad but only strange, and if you got to know them well with all their ins and outs and learnt to deal with them properly, neither too wilfully nor too indulgently, then many of them might easily be brought to their senses. After all, one servant did manage to do that with his master. Sometimes he could do nothing right by him and, as often happens in such situations, was blamed for many things that were not his fault.

Thus one day his master came home in a very bad mood and sat down to dinner. The soup was too hot or too cold for him, or neither; no matter, he was in a bad mood! So he picked up the dish and threw it and its contents out of the open window into the yard below. So what do you think the servant did? He didn't hesitate, he threw the meat he was bringing to table down into the yard after the soup, then the bread, the wine, and finally the tablecloth and everything on it, all down into the yard too. 'What the devil do you think you're doing?' said his master angrily and rose threateningly to his feet. But the servant replied quietly and calmly, 'Pardon me if I misunderstood your wishes. I thought you wanted to eat outside today. The air's warm, the sky's blue, and look how lovely the apple blossom is and how happy the bees are sipping at the flowers!' Never again would the soup go out through the window! His master saw he was wrong, cheered up at the sight of the beautiful spring day, smiled to himself at his man's quick thinking, and in his heart he was grateful to him for teaching him a lesson.

The Clever Judge

Not everything that happens in the East is so wrong. We are told the following event took place there. A rich man had been careless and lost a large sum of money sewn up in a cloth. He made his loss known, and in the usual way offered a reward for its return, in this case a hundred thalers. Soon a good honest man came to see him. 'I have found your money,' he said. 'This must be yours.' He had the open look of an upright fellow with a clear conscience, and that was good. The rich man looked happy too, but only at seeing his precious money again. As for his honesty, that we shall see! He counted the money and worked out quickly how he could cheat this man of the promised reward. 'My friend,' he said, 'there were in fact eight hundred thalers sewn up in this cloth. But I can find only seven hundred. So I take it you must have cut open a corner and taken your one hundred thalers' reward. You acted quite properly. I thank you!' That was not good. But we haven't got to the end yet. Honesty is the best policy, and wrongdoing never proves right. The honest man who had found the money and who was less concerned for his reward than for his blameless name protested that he had found the packet just as he handed it over, and had handed over exactly what he had found. In the end they appeared in court. Both of them stuck to their stories, one that eight hundred thalers were sewn up in the cloth, the other that he had left the packet just as he found it and had taken nothing from it. It was hard to know what to do. But the clever judge, who seemed from the outset to recognize the honesty of the one and the bad faith of the other, approached the problem as follows. He had both swear their statements on solemn oath, and then passed the following judgement: 'Since one of you lost eight hundred thalers and the other found a packet containing only seven hundred, the package found by that second party cannot be the one to which the first party has just claim. You, my honest friend, take back the money you found and put it into safe keeping until the person who lost only seven hundred thalers makes himself known. And you I can only advise to be patient until someone says he has found your eight hundred thalers.' That was his judgement, and that was final.

The Artful Hussar

A hussar in the last war knew that the farmer he met on the road
had just sold his hay for a hundred guilders and was on his way
home with the money. So he asked him for something to buy
tobacco and brandy. Who knows, he might have been happy with
a few coppers. But the farmer swore black and blue he had spent
his last kreuzer in the nearby village and had nothing left. 'If we
weren't so far from my quarters,' said the hussar, 'we could both
be helped out of this difficulty; but you have nothing, and neither
have I; so we'll just have to go to Saint Alphonsus! We'll share
what he gives us like brothers.' This Saint Alphonsus stood carved
from stone in an old, little frequented chapel in the fields. At first
the farmer was not too keen to make the pilgrimage. But the
hussar allowed no objection, and on the way he was so vigorous in
his assurances that Saint Alphonsus had never let him down when
in need that the farmer began to cherish hopes himself. So you
think the hussar's comrade and accomplice was hiding in the
deserted chapel, do you? Not a bit of it! No one was there, only
the stone figure of Alphonsus, and they knelt before him, and the
hussar appeared to be praying fervently. 'This is it!' he whispered
to the farmer, 'the saint has just beckoned to me.' He got to his
feet and went to put his ear to the lips of stone and came back
delighted. 'He's given me a guilder, he says it's in my purse!' And
indeed to the other's amazement the hussar took out a guilder,
but one that he had had there all the time, and shared it like a
brother as promised. That made sense to the farmer and he
agreed that the hussar should try again. All went just as before.
This time the hussar was even happier when he came back to the
farmer. 'Now Saint Alphonsus has given us a hundred guilders all

in one go! They're in your purse.' The farmer turned deadly white when he heard this and repeated his protests that he had no money at all. But the hussar persuaded him he must trust Saint Alphonsus and just take a look; Alfonsus had never deceived him! So whether he liked it or not he had to turn his pockets inside out and empty them. Then the hundred guilders appeared all right, and since he had taken half of the hussar's guilder it was no use pleading and imploring, he had to share his hundred.

That was all very artful and cunning, but that doesn't make it right, especially in a chapel.

The Mole

Of all the animals that suckle their young the mole is the only one that searches for its food alone in dark tunnels underground.

And that one fact is more than enough, some of you will say, and you're thinking of your fields and meadows, and how they are covered with molehills and the earth disturbed and riddled with holes, and how the plants above die off when that dastardly animal eats their roots down below!

So let's now bring the culprit to trial!

It's true and can't be denied that in certain places it disturbs and loosens the soil as it burrows its runs underground.

It is also true that the mounds it throws up cover much fertile ground, hinder the growth of the shoots underneath and can even smother them. Yet that can be put right by a diligent hand with a rake.

But which of you has seen a mole eating the roots? Who can say it does that?

Well, this is what people say: Wherever the roots are eaten and the plants die off, there you'll find moles; and where there are no moles it doesn't happen. So it must be the moles! Those who say that are presumably the same people who used to say: If the frogs croak early in spring the leaves will open early too; but if the frogs stay quiet the buds won't open; therefore the frogs' croaking opens the leaves! See how people can be wrong!

But we have now in this court a lawyer to speak in defence of moles, he's an experienced farmer and a naturalist, and he says:

'It's not the mole that eats the roots, but the grubs or white worms under ground which later change into cockchafers or other insects. The mole eats the grubs and rids the soil of these pests.'

So now we can see why moles are found wherever the grass and the plants are sickly and dying off: it is because they are after the grubs there. And then the mole is blamed for the damage done by the grubs and is rewarded with a curse and a death sentence for helping the farmer!

'That's another of those stories dreamt up indoors or read in books,' you'll be saying, 'by someone who has never set eyes on a mole!'

But wait a moment! The man we've just heard knows the mole better than any of you, better than your expert molecatchers, as you will see. For you can make two tests to check if he is telling the truth.

First, you can look at the mole's mouth. For all four-legged creatures or mammals made by nature to nibble at roots have in each jaw, upper and lower, just two sharp front teeth, and no eyeteeth at all, but a gap in front of the grinders. Whereas all beasts of prey that catch and eat other animals have six or more pointed front teeth, with eyeteeth on each side, and a row of grinders behind them. Now, if you inspect a mole's jaws you will find this: it has six sharp front teeth in the upper jaw and eight in the lower, and eyeteeth behind them on each side, top and bottom. That means it is not an animal that gnaws at roots but a small animal of prey that eats other animals.

Second, you can cut open the belly of a dead mole and see what is inside. What it eats must go into its belly, it must have eaten what's in its stomach! Now, if you make this test you'll never find anything like root fibres in the mole's stomach, but you will always find the skins of white worms, earthworms and other pests that live in the ground.

How does the case look now?

If you put yourself out to make life hard for moles and try to get rid of them then you are doing yourself great harm and the white worms a big favour. Then they can safely ravage your meadows and fields, they'll grow big and fat, and in spring the cockchafers will appear, eat your trees as bare as birch-brooms, and you'll have the devil to pay.

That's how the case stands!

The Dentist

Two loafers who had been roaming around the country together for some time because they were too lazy to work or had learnt no trade finally got into a tight corner because they had no money left, and they saw no quick way of getting any. Then they had this idea: they went begging at doors for bread which they intended to use, not to fill their stomachs, but to stage a trick. For they kneaded and rolled it into little balls and coated them with the dust from old, rotten worm-eaten wood so that they looked just like yellow pills from the chemist. Then for a couple of pence they bought some sheets of red paper at the bookbinder's (for a pretty colour often helps take people in). Next they cut up the paper and wrapped the pills in it, six or eight to a little packet. Then one of them went on ahead to a village where there was a fair and into the Red Lion where he hoped to find a good crowd. He ordered a glass of wine, but he didn't drink it but sat sadly in a corner holding his face in his hand, moaning under his breath and fidgeting and turning this way and that. The good farmers and townsfolk in the inn thought the poor fellow must have terrible toothache. Yet what could they do? They pitied him, they consoled him, saying it would soon go away, then went back to their drinks and their market-day affairs. Meanwhile the other idler came in. The two scoundrels pretended they had never seen each other in their lives before. They didn't look at each other until the one seemed to react to the other's moans in the corner. 'My friend,' he said, 'have you got toothache?' and he strode slowly over to him. 'I am Dr Schnauzius Rapunzius from Trafalgar,' he continued. Such resounding foreign names help take people in too, you know, like pretty colours. 'If you take my tooth pills,' he went on, 'I can easily get rid of the pain, one of them will do the trick, at most two.' 'Please God you're right!' said the other rogue. So now the fine doctor Rapunzius took one of the red packets from his pocket and prescribed one pill, to be placed on the tongue and bitten on firmly. The customers at the other tables now craned their necks and one by one they came over to observe the miracle cure. You can imagine what happened! But no, the first bite seemed to do the patient no good at all, he gave a terrible scream. The doctor was pleased! They had, he said, got the better of the pain, and quickly he gave him the second pill to be taken likewise. Now suddenly the pain had all gone. The patient jumped for joy, wiped the sweat from his brow, though there was none there, and pretended to show his thanks by pressing more than a trifling sum into his saviour's hand. The trick was artfully done and had its desired effect. For all those present now wanted some of these excellent pills too. The doctor offered them at twenty-four kreuzers a packet, and they were all sold in a few minutes. Of course the two scoundrels now left separately one after the other, met up to laugh at the people's stupidity, and had a good time on their money.

The fools had paid dear for a few crumbs of bread! Even in times of famine you never got so little for twenty-four kreuzers. But the waste of money was not the worst part of it. For in time the pellets of breadcrumbs naturally became as hard as stone. So when a year later a poor dupe had toothache and confidently bit on a pill with the offending tooth, once and then again, just imagine the awful pain that he had got himself for twenty-four kreuzers instead of a cure!

From this we can learn how easy it is to be tricked if you believe what is told you by any vagrant whom you meet for the first time in your life, have never seen before and will never see again. Some of you who read this will perhaps be thinking: 'I was once silly like that too and brought suffering on myself!'

Remember: Those who can, earn their money elsewhere and don't go around villages and fairs with holes in their stockings, or a white buckle on one shoe and a yellow one on the other.

Two Stories

How easily some people can be annoyed and lose their tempers over trifles, and how easily these same people can be brought to their senses by an unexpected quick-thinking reaction. That we saw in the example of the quick-witted servant whose master threw the soup out of the window. The following two stories teach a similar lesson.

A street urchin asked an elegantly dressed passer-by for a penny, and when he turned a deaf ear he promised to show him for a penny how you can get angry and abusive and violent. As you read this many of you will be saying to yourselves that's not worth a farthing let alone a penny, for abuse and violence are bad, not good at all! But it's worth more than you think! For if you know how something bad can come about you also know how to stop it happening. This man must have thought that too, for he gave the boy a penny. But the urchin now demanded another penny, and when he got that, a third and fourth, and finally a sixth. And when he wouldn't even then do his piece the man lost patience. He called the boy a shameless beggar, threatened to chase him off with his stick, and in the end he did indeed strike him more than once. 'You ill-mannered brute you,' cried the boy, 'you're old enough to know better! Didn't I promise to teach you how you get abusive and violent? Haven't you given me sixpence to do just that? Now you are violent, and you can see how that came about! So why are you hitting me?' Much as the good man disliked this turn of events he saw that the cunning lad was right and he was wrong. He calmed down, took it as a warning never to flare up like that again and thought the lesson he had been given was indeed worth sixpence.

A citizen in another town was hurrying down the street, looking very serious. You could tell he had something important to attend to. The town magistrate, who must have been a prying and quick-tempered man, was passing that way, the bailiff at his heels. 'Where are you off to in such a hurry?' he said to the citizen, who answered very calmly, 'Your Honour, I don't know that myself.' 'But you don't look as if you're just out for a stroll! You must have something important to attend to!' 'That may be,' the citizen continued, 'but I swear I don't know where I'm going.' The magistrate was now greatly annoyed. Perhaps he also suspected that the man was up to no good and couldn't admit it. Anyway, in all seriousness he threatened to take him straight off the street into prison if he wouldn't say where he was going. But that got him nowhere, and in the end the magistrate really did order the bailiff to take this obstinate fellow away. But then the man, who had his wits about him, said, 'Now, Your Honour, you can see that I was telling the truth! How could I have known a minute ago that I was on the way to jail? And can I be certain even now that that's where I'm going?' 'No, you can't,' said the magistrate, 'and you shan't go to jail!' The citizen's quick-thinking response brought the magistrate to his senses. He secretly reproached himself for being so testy, and let the man go on his way.

It is after all worth remembering that a person who seems quite ordinary can still now and again teach a lesson to someone who thinks himself marvellously wise and sensible.

Settling Accounts with a Ghost

In a certain village that I could name there's a path through the churchyard which then goes over a field belonging to the man who lives next to the church, and it's a right of way. But whenever it rained and the field paths became slippery quagmires, people would walk a yard or two to the side and trample on the growing crop, so that when it rained for some time the path grew wider and the field smaller, and there was nothing right about that! Up to a point the owner was able to do something about it. In daytime, if he wasn't busy at something else, he kept a strict lookout, and when a stupid fellow came along this path, one who cared more for his shoes than his neighbour's barley, he rushed out and made him pay a forfeit or settled the matter on the spot by boxing his ears. But at night when there was most need for a good firm path underfoot things only got worse, and each time he marked the path with sticks and brushwood, within a few nights they were all pulled out or kicked over, and some people may have done it on purpose. But then something unusual came to his aid. Suddenly the churchyard through which the path passed became unsafe. Several times on dry starlit nights a tall white ghost was seen walking over the graves. When it rained or was pitch black a fearful groaning and whining was heard, or a rattling in the charnel house as if all the skulls and skeletons were coming back to life. Those who heard it all ran trembling back out through the nearest gate, and soon once dusk had fallen and the last swallow had disappeared from the sky no one was to be seen on the path in the churchyard, until one day a level-headed and plucky man from one of the nearby villages was held up in this village and took the shortest way home over the notorious churchyard and the barley field. For though his friends warned him of the danger and tried to dissuade him, he said finally, 'If it is a ghost, God knows I am taking the quickest way home to my wife and children, I've done nothing wrong, and a ghost, even if it's the worst of the lot, cannot harm me. But if it's flesh and blood then I've got a pair of fists and know how to use them!' So he set off. But as he was going through the churchyard and had just passed the second gravestone he heard a piteous moaning and groaning behind him, and when he looked round, there behind him, as if from one of the graves, rose a tall pale shape. The moon shone wanly on the tombstones. It was deathly quiet all around, only a couple of bats fluttered by. Our good man didn't feel so sure of himself now, as he afterwards admitted, and he would gladly have turned around if that had not meant going back past the ghost. So what was he to do? He walked on slowly and silently between the graves and past several black crosses. To his horror, slowly, and still groaning, the ghost followed him to the edge of the churchyard, and that was as it should be, and then out of the churchyard, and that was silly.

But that's how things are. However sly a trickster, he always gives himself away. For as soon as our good man saw the ghost on the field he thought to himself: a proper ghost should remain at his post like a sentry, a spirit that belongs in the graveyard doesn't go on to the farmer's field! So suddenly his courage returned, he whisked round and with one hand grabbed hold of the white figure and immediately realized that he was gripping a shirt under a sheet and in it was a fellow who hadn't yet taken up permanent residence in the graveyard. So with his other hand he set about giving him a thrashing until he grew tired of the sport, and since he couldn't see where he was hitting under the sheet the poor ghost had to take a random beating.

That was the end of the story and no more was heard of the matter, except that the owner of the barley field was black and blue in the face for a couple of weeks, and from that time on there was no ghost to be seen in the churchyard. You see, the likes of our sturdy gentleman, they are the only true exorcists, and it would be nice if every other trickster and fraud were to meet his match and get his deserts in the same way.

A Short Stage

The postmaster told a Jew who drove up to his relay station with two horses, 'From here on you'll have to take three! It's a hard pull uphill and the surface is still soft. But that way you'll be there in three hours.' The Jew asked, 'When will I get there if I take four?' 'In two hours.' 'And if I take six?' 'In one hour.' 'I'll tell you what,' said the Jew after a while, 'Harness up eight. That way I shan't have to set off at all!'

The Careful Dreamer

There certainly are some silly people in this world of ours!

Once a stranger was spending the night in the little town of Witlisbach in the canton of Berne, and when he was going to bed and was already undressed but for his shirt he took a pair of slippers from his pack, put them on, tied them to his feet with his garters and climbed into bed thus shod. Another traveller, with whom he was sharing the room that night, said to him, 'My dear fellow, why on earth are you doing that?' 'Just in case!' was the reply. 'You see, once I dreamt I trod on broken glass. And it hurt me so much in my sleep that nothing will ever persuade me to go to bed barefoot again.'

A Bad Win

A young fellow was boasting to a Jew how he could wield a knife with such accuracy he could split a pin lengthwise with one blow. 'Cross my heart, Brother Abraham,' he said, 'I bet you half a sovereign I can trim back the black edge of your nail down to a hair's breadth from two feet away and not spill a drop of blood!' The bet was accepted, for the Jew didn't think it possible, and the money put down on the table. The young fellow drew his knife and brought it down – and lost, for with one clumsy swipe he cut the poor Jew's nail clean off, the black bit and the white bit, and the top finger joint with it. The Jew gave a loud shriek, took the money and said: 'Alas, I have won!'

All those who are tempted to risk more than they stand to gain should think of this Jew!

How many of those who rushed to take their disputes to law might have said the same thing! Once a general announced his victory to his monarch with these words: 'If I win another victory like this one I shall be the only one to come back home!' He too meant: Alas, I have won!

Strange Reckoning at the Inn

Sometimes a cheeky trick comes off, sometimes it costs you your coat, often your skin as well. But in this case it was only coats. One day, you see, three merry students on their travels didn't have a brass farthing left between them, they had spent everything on a good time, but nevertheless they went into another inn intending to leave without sneaking out by the back door, and it suited them fine that they found only the landlord's nice young wife inside. They ate and drank merrily and talked very learnedly about the world being many thousands of years old and how it would last as long again, and how each year, to the day and the hour, everything that happened came to pass as it had done on that day and at that hour six thousand years before. Eventually one of them turned to the landlady, who was sitting on one side by the window knitting and listening attentively, and said, 'That's how it is, ma'am, we've had to learn that from our learned tomes.' And one had the impudence to assert that he just about remembered their being there six thousand years ago, and he remembered the landlady's pretty friendly face very well indeed. They carried on talking for some time, and the more the landlady seemed to believe everything they said the more the young gadabouts tucked into the wine and the meat and a fistful of pretzels, and in the end their bill stood chalked up at five guilders and sixteen kreuzers. They had eaten and drunk their fill, and now they came out with the trick they had planned.

'Ma'am,' said one, 'this time we are short of money, for there are so many inns on the road. But since we know you're a clever woman we hope that as old friends we can have credit here, and if you agree, in six thousand years' time when we come again we'll pay our old bill together with the new one.' The sensible landlady was not upset by that, it was fine by her, she was delighted that the young gentlemen were well served. But before they had noticed her move she was standing in front of the door and was asking the gentlemen kindly just to settle now the bill of five guilders and sixteen kreuzers that they owed from six thousand years ago, since, as they said, everything that happened now was an exact repetition of what had taken place before. Unfortunately just at that moment the village mayor came in with a couple of sturdy men to enjoy a glass of wine together. That didn't suit our gay young dogs at all! For now the official verdict was pronounced and carried out: you had to give it to someone who had allowed credit for six thousand years! The gentlemen were therefore to pay their old debt immediately or leave their newish overcoats as a pledge. They were obliged to take the second option, and the landlady promised to return their coats in six thousand years' time when they came again with a bit more money.

This took place in 1805 on the 17th of April in the inn at Segringen.

A Strange Walk and Ride

A man was riding home on his donkey, with his son walking alongside on foot. A passer-by came up and said, 'That's not right, you shouldn't be riding and making your son walk! Your legs are stronger than his!' So he got down from the donkey and let his son ride. Now another passer-by came up and said, 'That's not right, young fellow, you shouldn't be riding and making your father walk! Your legs are younger than his!' So they both sat on the donkey and rode on a little way. Now a third passer-by came up and said, 'What nonsense is this? Two men on a frail animal! I've a good mind to take a stick to you both and knock you off its back!' So the two of them got down, and all three of them went on on foot, father and son to right and left, the donkey in the middle. Now a fourth passer-by came up and said, 'A queer threesome you make! Must all of you tire yourselves out walking? Surely it's easier if one of you saves his legs?' So the father tied the donkey's two front legs together and the son tied its back legs and they found a strong branch by the roadside and carried the donkey home slung between their shoulders.

That's what can happen if you try to please everybody!

An Unusual Apology

The remarkable thing is that a scoundrel isn't at all pleased to be called an honest man, he only takes it as a greater insult.

Two men were sitting in the inn in a nearby village. One of them had a thoroughly bad name, and he was as welcome as a polecat in anybody's back yard! But nothing could be proved against him in court. The other man quarrelled with him in this inn, and in his anger and because a glass of wine too many had gone to his head he said to him, 'You scoundrel!' For one of that kind that should be enough. But this fellow wasn't satisfied, he wanted more, returned the abuse and demanded proof. So one word led to another and to 'You thief! You robber!' And still he wasn't satisfied and took the case to the magistrate. Now, of course, the man who had heaped the insults on him was in a fix. He didn't want to eat his words, but he couldn't prove they were justified because he had no witnesses to bear out what he knew, so he had to pay a fine of a guilder for calling an honest man a rogue and to apologize to him, and he thought to himself: That glass of wine cost me dear! But when he had paid the fine he said, 'So, Your Honour, it costs you a guilder if you call an honest man a rogue, does it? What then does it cost you if absent-mindedly, say, or for some other reason, you call a rogue an honest man?'

The magistrate smiled and said, 'It costs nothing, that's no insult.' So now the accused turned to his adversary and said, 'I am sorry, my honest friend! Forgive me, my honest fellow! Goodbye, honest man!' Hearing this, his opponent, knowing full well how it was meant, complained angrily that this only added to the previous insult. But the magistrate, who must after all have known he was a suspicious character, told him he could demand no further satisfaction.

Unexpected Reunion

At Falun in Sweden, a good fifty years ago, a young miner kissed his pretty young bride-to-be and said, 'On the feast of Saint Lucia the parson will bless our love and we shall be man and wife and start a home of our own.' 'And may peace and love dwell there with us,' said his lovely bride, and smiled sweetly, 'for you are everything to me, and without you I'd sooner be in the grave than anywhere else.' When however, before the feast of Saint Lucia, the parson had called out their names in church for the second time: 'If any of you know cause, or just hindrance, why these two persons should not be joined together in holy Matrimony' – Death paid a call. For the next day when the young man passed her house in his black miner's suit (a miner is always dressed ready for his own funeral), he tapped at the window as usual and wished her good morning all right, but he did not wish her good evening. He did not return from the mine, and in vain that same morning she sewed a red border on a black neckerchief for him to wear on their wedding day, and when he did not come back she put it away, and she wept for him, and never forgot him.

In the meantime the city of Lisbon in Portugal was destroyed by an earthquake, the Seven Years War came and went, the Emperor Francis I died, the Jesuits were dissolved, Poland was partitioned, the Empress Maria Theresa died, and Struensee was executed, and America became independent, and the combined French and Spanish force failed to take Gibraltar. The Turks cooped up General Stein in the Veterane Cave in Hungary, and the Emperor Joseph died too. King Gustavus of Sweden conquered Russian Finland, the French Revolution came and the long war began, and the Emperor Leopold II too was buried. Napoleon defeated Prussia, the English bombarded Copenhagen, and the farmers sowed and reaped. The millers ground the corn, the blacksmiths wielded their hammers, and the miners dug for seams of metal in their workplace under the ground.*

But in 1809, within a day or two of the feast of Saint John, when the miners at Falun were trying to open up a passage between two shafts, they dug out from the rubble and the vitriol water, a good three hundred yards below ground, the body of a young man soaked in ferrous vitriol but otherwise untouched by decay and unchanged, so that all his features and his age were still clearly recognizable, as if he had died only an hour before or had just nodded off at work. Yet when they brought him to the surface his father and mother and friends and acquaintances were all long since dead, and no one claimed to know the sleeping youth or to remember his misadventure, until the woman came who had once been promised to the miner who one day had gone below and had not returned. Grey and bent, she hobbled up on a crutch to where he lay and recognized her bridegroom; and, more in joyous rapture than in grief, she sank down over the beloved corpse, and it was some time before she had recovered from her fervent emotion. 'It is my betrothed,' she

said at last, 'whom I have mourned these past fifty years, and now God grants that I see him once more before I die. A week before our wedding he went under ground and never came up again.' The hearts of all those there were moved to sadness and tears when they saw the former bride-to-be as an old woman whose beauty and strength had left her, and the groom still in the flower of his youth; and how the flame of young love was rekindled in her breast after fifty years, yet he did not open his mouth to smile, nor his eyes to recognize her; and how finally she, as the sole relative and the only person who had claim to him, had the miners carry him into her house until his grave was made ready for him in the churchyard.

The next day when the grave lay ready in the churchyard and the miners came to fetch him she opened a casket and put the black silk neckerchief with the red stripes on him, and then she went with him in her best Sunday dress, as if it were her wedding day, not the day of his burial. You see, as they lowered him into his grave in the churchyard she said, 'Sleep well for another day or a week or so longer in your cold wedding bed, and don't let time weigh heavy on you! I have only a few things left to do, and I shall join you soon, and soon the day will dawn.'

'What the earth has given back once it will not withhold again at the final call', she said as she went away and looked back over her shoulder once more.

The Great Sanhedrin in Paris*

That the Jews have lived without a homeland and without citizens' rights since the destruction of Jerusalem, that is for more than 1,700 years, and have been dispersed over all the earth; that most of them live on the labour of the other inhabitants without doing useful work themselves and are therefore also frequently despised, abused as aliens and persecuted: God knows this is a sorry state of affairs! Many in their folly therefore say, 'They should all be driven out of our land!' Others are more sensible and say, 'They should be kept here in useful employment.'

The great Emperor Napoleon made a start on this. What he decreed and arranged for the Jews in France and the Kingdom of Italy is worth noting, now and in the future.

Already in the Revolution all the Jews who lived in France were given French citizenship and were addressed without further ado as Citizen Aaron, Citizen Levi and Citizen Rabbi, and people shook them by the hand as brothers. But what did that amount to? Christian citizens have one set of laws, Jewish citizens have another and don't want to mix with the goys. But two laws and two wills in one body of citizens work like a whirlpool in a stream. The water tries to go both ways, and a mill at that spot doesn't grind much corn.

The great Emperor Napoleon understood that all right, and in 1806, before setting out on his long journey to Jena, Berlin, Warsaw and Eylau,* he had letters sent to all the Jews in France telling them to choose men of good sense and learning from their midst to come to him from all the regions of the empire. Now everyone wondered what that meant, one said this and another said that, for instance that the Emperor intended to send the Jews back to their old homeland on the mountain of Lebanon, by the river of Egypt and by the sea.

But when the representatives and rabbis from all the regions where the Jews lived had come together, the Emperor put certain questions to them which they were to turn over in their hearts and answer according to the law, and it was clear that it wasn't a matter of being banished from the country, but of staying there and of forging strong ties between the Jews and the other citizens in France and the Kingdom of Italy. For all the questions amounted to whether a Jew's faith allowed him to regard the country where he lived as his homeland and its other citizens as his fellow citizens, and to keep the civil laws of that land.

Now it seemed there could be a catch in this so that neither yes nor no was a good answer. But the representatives tell us the spirit of divine wisdom shone within them and their answer was pleasing in the eyes of the Emperor.

So this gathering of Jews formed itself into the Great Sanhedrin, and that was an amazing wonder in our own times. For the Great Sanhedrin is not an outsize Jew in Paris, like the giant Goliath, who was a Philistine anyway, but sanhedrin means a gathering and was the name of the High Council in Jerusalem in the old times long ago. It consisted of seventy-one men who were considered the most sensible and wisest in the whole nation, and their pronouncements on the law were accepted and applied throughout Israel.

The representatives of the Jews reinstated such a Council, saying there had been no Great Sanhedrin for fifteen hundred years until this one under the protection of the illustrious Emperor Napoleon.

These are the laws proclaimed by the Great Sanhedrin in Paris in the year 5567 after the creation of the world, in the month of Adar of that year, on the 22nd day of that month:

1) Jewish marriage shall be of one man and one woman. No Israelite may have more than one wife at one time.

2) No rabbi may declare a married couple divorced unless the secular authorities have previously announced the marriage dissolved according to the civil law.

3) No rabbi may confirm a marriage unless the couple have previously been declared fit to marry by the secular authorities. But a Jew may marry a Christian's daughter and a Christian the daughter of a Jew. That is no impediment.

4) The Great Sanhedrin acknowledges that Christians and Jews are brothers because they worship one God who created heaven and earth, and it therefore commands Israelites to live with Frenchmen and Italians and the subjects of any land where they dwell as with brothers and fellow citizens if they acknowledge and honour the same one God.

5) Every Israelite shall as commanded in the Law of Moses use justice and neighbourly love towards Christians because they are his brothers, as well as towards those of his own faith, within France and the Kingdom of Italy and elsewhere.

6) The Great Sanhedrin recognizes the country in which an Israelite is born and brought up, or where he has settled and enjoys the protection of the laws, to be his homeland, and commands all Israelites in France and the Kingdom of Italy to look upon that country as their homeland, to serve and defend it, etc. Jewish soldiers, while serving as soldiers, are released from those observances not reconcilable with the military life.

7) The Great Sanhedrin commands all Israelites to bring up their children to love work and to encourage them to take up useful skills and trades, and urges Israelites to acquire fixed property and to renounce all activities that might cause them to be despised or hated by their fellow citizens.

8) No Israelite may charge interest on money lent to the head of a Jewish family in need; that loan is an act of charity; but capital invested in business may earn interest.

9) The same applies to money lent to citizens of other religions. All usury is forbidden, in France and the Kingdom of Italy and elsewhere, not only in dealings with fellow believers and fellow citizens but also with foreigners.

These nine articles were published on the 2nd of March 1807 and signed by the president of the Great Sanhedrin, Rabbi D. Sinzheim of Strassburg, and other High Councillors.

The Sly Pilgrim

A few years ago an idler roamed around the countryside pretending to be a pious pilgrim, saying he came from Paderborn and was making for the Holy Sepulchre in Jerusalem, and already at the Coach and Horses in Müllheim he was asking, 'How far is it to Jerusalem now?' They told him, 'Seven hundred hours. But you'll save a quarter of an hour if you take the path to Mauchen.' So he went by way of Mauchen to save himself a quarter of an hour on his long journey. That wasn't such a bad idea. You must not scorn a small gain or a bigger one won't come your way. You more often get a chance to save or make threepence than a florin. But eight threepennies make a florin, and if on a journey of seven hundred hours you can save a quarter of an hour every five hours, over the whole journey you will save – now, who can work that out? How many hours? But that wasn't how our supposed pilgrim saw it! Since he was only after an easy life and a good meal he didn't care which way he went. As the old saying goes, a beggar can never take the wrong turning, it's a poor village indeed where he can't collect more than the cost of the shoe leather he has worn out on the road, especially if he goes barefoot. Yet our pilgrim intended to get back as soon as he could to the main road where he'd find rich people's houses and good cooking. For this rascal wasn't content, as a true pilgrim should be, with common food given in compassion by a pious hand, he wanted nothing but nourishing pebble soup! You see, whenever he saw a nice inn by the road, for instance the Post House at Krozingen or the Basel Arms at Schliengen, he would go in and very humbly and hungrily ask for a nice soup made of pebbles and water, in God's name, he had no money. And when the innkeeper's wife took pity on him and said, 'Pious pilgrim, pebbles are not easy to digest!', he said, 'That's just it! Pebbles last longer than bread and it's a long way to Jerusalem. But if you were to give me a little glass of wine too, in God's name, it would help me digest them.' Now if she said, 'But good pilgrim, a soup like that won't give you any strength at all!' then he replied, 'Well, if you use broth instead of water then of course it would be more nourishing.' And when she brought him his broth and said, 'The bits at the bottom are still a bit hard, I'm afraid,' then he'd say, 'You're right, and the broth looks a little thin. Would you have a couple of spoonfuls of vegetables to add to it, or a scrap of meat, or maybe both?' If now the innkeeper's wife still felt sorry for him and put some meat and vegetables in the bowl, he said, 'God bless you! Now just hand me a piece of bread and I'll tuck into your soup!' Then he would push back the sleeves of his pilgrim's habit, sit down and set to work with relish, and when he had eaten the last crumb of bread, drained the wine, and finished the last morsel of meat and vegetables and the last drop of broth, he would wipe his mouth on the tablecloth or his sleeve, or perhaps he wouldn't bother, and he'd say, 'Missus, your soup has strengthened me as a good soup should, what a shame I can't find room for the nice pebbles now! But put them by, and when I come back I'll bring you a holy conch from the seashore at Ascalon or a Jericho rose.'

Treachery Gets Its Just Reward

When in the war between France and Prussia* part of the French Army moved into Silesia, troops from the Confederation of the Rhine* were there with them, and an officer from Bavaria or Württemberg was quartered on a nobleman and was given a room hung with many very fine and valuable paintings. The officer seemed delighted, and when he had been in the house several days and was treated very kindly there, he asked his host to make him a gift of one of these pictures. The nobleman said he would be glad to, and left it to the officer to choose the one he liked best.

Well now, if you are allowed to choose your own present, common sense and good manners demand that you don't take the best and most valuable thing on offer, and that's not what is meant. This officer seemed to be aware of this, for of all the paintings he chose one of the least impressive. Yet our Silesian noble was not happy with that and pressed him to take the most valuable one instead. 'My dear colonel,' he said, clearly ill at ease, 'why must you choose the worst one, and one that I'm attached to for other reasons too? Won't you take this one here, or that one over there!' But the officer wouldn't listen to him, and seeming not to notice that his host was growing more and more anxious he took down the painting he had chosen. And there, on the wall where it had hung, was a large damp patch. 'What's this?' said the officer to the nobleman who was now as white as a sheet, and he sounded angry, and he poked at the wall and a couple of newly laid and freshly painted bricks fell out, and behind them was hidden all the nobleman's money, gold and silver. He thought he had lost it all now. He expected the enemy soldier to take a large part of it at least, without making an inventory or recording the deal, he was resigned to that outcome and asked him only how he knew that the money was hidden behind the picture. The officer answered, 'I'll call in my informant at once, I owe him a reward anyway,' and soon his servant led in – would you believe it? – the master bricklayer himself, the one who had bricked up the hole in the wall and had been paid for it.

Now that is one of the most dastardly tricks the devil can chalk up on anyone's list of sins. For a tradesman owes it to be loyal to his customers and to keep quiet about their affairs, provided they are not wrong or unlawful, just as if he was sworn to an oath of secrecy.

But what won't people do for money! Often exactly what they

do to earn a good beating or a stretch in jail or on the gallows, though those are very different goals! Our master craftsman and scoundrel was to discover this. For the worthy officer had him taken outside and paid on the spot with one hundred strokes, good coins of the realm all of them, not one of them a fake. But he returned the nobleman's property to him untouched.

Let's applaud both deeds and wish that everyone who has a soldier quartered on him receives such an honest guest, and that every act of treachery gets a similar reward.

Mixed Fortunes

Seldom have good and bad luck come together in so curious a way as in the fate of two sailors during the last war at sea between the Russians and the Turks.* In one battle things got pretty hot, for cannon balls came whistling past, planks and masts splintered, fireballs flew, and now one ship, now another, started to burn and there was no putting out the flames. It must be terrible to have no choice but to jump to one's death in the water or be burnt alive! But our two Russian tars were spared that choice. The powder chamber on their ship caught fire and a terrible explosion blew the vessel to pieces. These two sailors were shot up skywards, they turned somersaults over each other high in the air and then fell back down into the sea just behind the enemy fleet, and they were alive still and unhurt, and that was a stroke of good fortune! But the Turks were sailing towards them, they hauled them like drowned rats out of the water and took them on board; and since they were enemies their welcome was a brief one. Nobody wasted much time asking if they had eaten before they set off from the Russian fleet, but put them in chains in the damp, dark ship's hold, and that was bad luck! Meanwhile cannon balls were still whistling overhead, planks and masts splintered, fireballs flew, and whoosh! now the Turkish ship with the two prisoners on board blew up too and shot skywards in a thousand pieces. The sailors went up with it and dropped back into the water again alongside the Russian fleet, were quickly pulled out by their friends, and they were still alive, and that was a great stroke of good fortune! But these two fine men had to pay for their release from captivity and for their double escape from death with a great sacrifice, for they each lost both their legs. They had been broken or horribly mangled when they were blown out of their chains as the Turkish ship exploded, and as soon as the battle was over they had to be amputated below the knee, and that was a terrible misfortune again! But both survived the operation and lived on for some years with only stumps of legs. In the end they died, first one and then the other, and after all they had experienced that wasn't the worst thing to have happened.

This story is told by a man who can be believed and who saw both the legless sailors himself and heard their tale from their own mouths.

The Commandant and the Light Infantry in Hersfeld

In the last campaign in Prussia and Russia* when the French Army and a large part of the allied troops were in Poland and Prussia, a contingent of the Baden Light Infantry was in Hessen and stationed at Hersfeld. For the Emperor had taken that state at the beginning of the campaign and stationed troops there. The inhabitants who preferred the way things had been before defied the new order and there were several acts of lawlessness, particularly in the town of Hersfeld. In one incident a French officer was killed. The French Emperor was engaged face to face with great numbers of the enemy and couldn't allow hostilities behind his back or let a spark spread into a great fire. The unfortunate people of Hersfeld thus had cause to regret their rashness. For the Emperor ordered the town to be looted, set alight at each corner and burnt to the ground.

This town of Hersfeld has many factories and thus many

rich inhabitants and fine buildings; and all of us with a heart can understand how its unfortunate people, those fathers and mothers with families, felt when they heard the dreadful news. The poor whose possessions could be carried off in one pair of arms were just as much affected as the rich whose goods couldn't all be loaded on a train of wagons. Great houses on the town square and small dwellings in the alleyways are all the same when burnt to the ground, just like rich and poor in the graveyard.

But the worst didn't happen. The French Commandant in Kassel and Hersfeld interceded and the punishment was reduced. Only four houses were to be burnt down, and that was lenient. But the plundering was to take place as ordered, and that was hard enough. The wretched townsfolk, hearing this latest decision, were so cowed and robbed of all presence of mind that the benevolent Commandant himself had to urge them, instead of weeping and pleading in vain, to remove their most precious possessions in the short time that was left. The dreadful hour arrived, the drums sounded over the wails of anguish. The soldiers hurried to their place of assembly through the crowds fleeing in despair. Then the stalwart Commandant of Hersfeld stood before the ranks of the infantry, and first he painted a vivid picture of the sad fate of the townspeople, then he said, 'Men, you now have permission to loot! Those who wish to take part, fall out!' Not one man moved. Not a single one! The order was repeated. Not one pair of boots stirred, and if the Commandant had intended the town to be plundered he would have had to do it himself. But no one was more pleased than he was that things turned out as they did, that is easy to tell. When the townsfolk learnt this, it was as if they woke from a bad dream. No one can describe their joy. They sent a delegation to the Commandant to

thank him for his kindness and magnanimity, and offered him a handsome gift to mark their gratitude. Who knows what they might not have done! But the Commandant refused and said he wouldn't be paid for a good deed.

This happened in Hersfeld in the year 1807, and the town is still standing.

Kannitverstan

All of us surely have daily occasion, in small places like Emmendingen and Gundelfingen as well as in Amsterdam, to contemplate if we are so minded the transience of earthly things, and to find contentment in our lot even if we don't live in a land flowing with milk and honey. But it was by the strangest roundabout way, in Amsterdam, and all because of a mistake, that a young German who was learning his trade encountered and recognized the truth. For when he arrived in that great and rich city of commerce full of splendid houses, swaying ships and industrious people, he was immediately struck by a large and handsome building whose like he had not yet seen all along the road from Duttlingen to Amsterdam. He gazed long and with amazement at this sumptuous mansion, the six chimneys on its roof, the fine cornices, and the tall windows each larger than the door of his father's house at home. In the end he could not refrain from addressing a passer-by. 'My good friend,' he said, 'could you tell me the name of the gentleman who owns this marvellous house with its window boxes full of tulips, daffodils and stocks?' But the man, who probably had more important things to do and who unfortunately understood as much German as the questioner Dutch, namely none at all, paused only to snap 'Kannitverstan' before hurrying on. This was a Dutch word, or really three words, meaning 'I can't understand you'. But our good fellow in foreign parts thought this was the name he wanted to know. 'He must be a very rich man, this Herr Kannitverstan', he thought, and walked on. Passing in and out of many streets he eventually came to the inlet of the sea that is there called Het Ey, which means The Y. Here were row upon row of ships, mast after mast, and at first he wondered how he, with just his two eyes, could possibly take in all these marvels, until after a while his gaze remained on one great ship which had arrived from the East Indies and was now unloading. Long lines of crates and bales were already piled up on the quay. More were still being rolled out, together with casks full of sugar and coffee, rice and pepper, with – excusez moi – mouse droppings among it. He watched for some time and then asked a man who was carrying a crate on his shoulder the name of the fortunate person for whom the sea brought all these goods ashore. 'Kannitverstan,' was the reply. So now he thought, 'Aha, so that's how it is! It's no wonder. If the sea delivers a man these riches he can easily build such houses on this earth and put tulips in gilded pots at his windows!' Now he retraced his steps, and his thoughts were sad indeed as he contemplated how poor a man he was among so many rich people in the world. But as he was thinking, 'If only I were as fortunate as this Herr Kannitverstan', he turned a corner and came across a great funeral procession. Slowly and sadly four horses decked in black were drawing a hearse, likewise draped in black, as if they knew they were bringing a dead man to his resting place. A long train of the deceased's friends and acquaintances followed behind, two by two, shrouded in black cloaks, silent. In the distance a lone bell tolled. Now our stranger was seized by that feeling of melancholy which is spared no one whose heart is in the right place when he sees a funeral, and he stood reverently hat in hand until they had all passed by. But he went up to the last person in the procession, who was calculating what he could make from his cotton if the price increased by ten guilders a hundredweight, took him gently by the sleeve and sincerely begged his pardon. 'That gentleman,' he said, 'for whom the bell tolls, must have been a good friend of yours, you walk behind so downcast and so deep in thought.' 'Kannitverstan,' came the reply. Then a pair of large tears welled from the eyes of our good young man from Duttlingen, and he was at once heavy at heart and yet easier in spirit too. 'Poor Kannitverstan!' he cried, 'what can all your riches bring you now? No more than my poverty will bring me one day: a shroud and a winding sheet; and of all your lovely flowers a bunch of rosemary perhaps on your cold breast, or a sprig of rue.' With these thoughts he followed the cortège as if he were part of it, right up to the graveside, watched the supposed Herr Kannitverstan lowered into his place of rest, and was more moved by the Dutch oration at the graveside, of which he understood not a word, than by many a sermon in German to which he paid little attention. Finally, with a light heart, he left with the others, made a hearty meal of a portion of Limburg cheese in an inn where they spoke German, and whenever again he was inclined to feel depressed because so many people in the world were so rich and he so poor he just remembered Herr Kannitverstan of Amsterdam, his great mansion, his ship laden with riches, and his narrow grave.

A Poor Reward

When in the last Prussian war* the French came to Berlin where the King of Prussia resides, a great deal of the royal property as well as other people's was taken and carried off or sold. For war brings nothing, it only takes. Much was claimed as booty, however well it was hidden they found it, but not everything. A large store of royal building timber remained undiscovered and untouched for some time. But eventually a rascal among the king's own subjects thought, there's a fair penny to be made here, and with a smirk and a wink he went to tell the French commandant what a lovely stack of oak and pine logs was still at such and such a place, and it was worth a few thousand guilders. But the French commandant paid him badly for this betrayal and said, 'Just you leave those fine logs where they are! There's no call to deprive the enemy of his most basic needs. For when your king returns he will need timber for new gallows for trusty subjects like you!'

Your Family Friend can only applaud that, and he would make a present of a few logs from his own coppice if they were needed.

He Speaks German!

As everyone knows there are many in the French Army who were born German, but they don't always let on in the field or in their quarters. That can be a real problem for a householder who knows no French and takes the soldier who has been quartered on him to be a regular Frenchman. But a citizen of Salzwedel who had an Alsatian lodged on him in the last war* chanced upon a quick way of getting to the bottom of it. The Alsatian's parley was all foutre diables, with sword in hand he was forever demanding something, now this, now that, and his host couldn't tell what it was he wanted. He would gladly have given him whatever it was if that had been possible. In desperation he ran next door to his cousin who knew a bit of French and asked for his help. The cousin said, 'He'll be from the Dauphiné, I'll sort it out all right!' But not at all! Things were bad before, now they were worse still. The Alsatian made demands the good man couldn't satisfy, until in the end he lost his temper and said, 'He's the biggest damned rascal the quarters' clerk ever sent to plague me!' But hardly had he uttered these rash words than he was given a terrible box on the ears by this would-be regular Frenchman. At that the neighbour said, 'Cousin, there's no need to be scared of him any more, he speaks German!'

Suvorov

We must be able to exercise control over ourselves, for without that no one can act properly and be worthy of respect. And once we have recognized what is right we must do it, not just once but always!

The Russian general Suvorov, who is well known to the Turks and Poles, the Italians and the Swiss,* was a hard and strict ruler of men. But his greatest quality was this, that he obeyed his own orders as if he was someone else and not Suvorov himself, and very often his adjutants had to order him in his own name to do this or that, and then he obeyed them at once. On one occasion he was carried away by anger at a soldier who was guilty of some misdemeanour or other and straight away set about giving him a thrashing. An adjutant plucked up his courage, thinking he could do the general and the soldier a good turn, hurried over and said: 'General Suvorov has ordered that no one is to lose his temper!' Suvorov stopped at once and said: 'The general's orders must be obeyed!'

The Stranger in Memel

Fact is often weirder than fiction. A stranger learnt that when some years ago he came by ship from the West Indies to the Baltic coast. At that time the Russian Emperor was visiting the King of Prussia. Both their majesties were standing together on the shore in ordinary clothes, without entourage, arm in arm like two very good friends. That's not something you see every day of the week! The new arrival didn't expect anything like that, and he went up to them all unsuspecting, thinking they were two merchants or well-to-do men from the locality, and struck up a conversation with them, curious to know everything that had happened while he had been abroad. Eventually, as the two monarchs spoke very affably with him, he was able politely to ask one of them who he was. 'I'm the King of Prussia.' Our stranger found that a little strange. Yet it's possible, he thought, and bowed respectfully to the King. And that was sensible. For when in doubt it is best to take the safest course and be polite in error rather than rude. Yet when the King continued, 'This is His Majesty, the Russian Emperor,' the good man thought a couple of wags were out to pull his leg and he said, 'If you two want to make a fool of an honest fellow, try it on with someone else! I didn't come back all the way from the West Indies to be made a fool of by you!' The Emperor tried to say that he really was the Tsar. But the stranger wouldn't listen to any more. 'You're a Russian clown more likely!' he said. But later when he told his story in the Old Oak he was put right and he went back and humbly begged their pardon, and the generous rulers forgave him a natural mistake, and afterwards they thought it a great joke.

An Odd Prescription

There's not usually anything very funny about taking a prescription to the chemist's. But once many years ago it was funny. One day a man from a remote farm drew up his cart drawn by two oxen in front of the town apothecary's and carefully unloaded a large pine door and carried it in. The apothecary raised his eyebrows and said, 'What are you doing here, my friend, with your parlour door? The carpenter lives two houses along on the left!' The man told him the doctor had come to his sick wife and wanted to prescribe medicine for her, but there was no pen, ink or paper in the house, only a piece of chalk. So the doctor wrote the prescription on the parlour door. So please, would the apothecary now kindly make up the potion for him?

That's how it happened, and let's hope it did her good! Resourcefulness is called for in an emergency.

The Barber's Boy at Segringen

You must not tempt God, but not people either. You see, last autumn a stranger came into the inn at Segringen, a soldier with a good growth of beard on him, and he looked rather odd and not to be trusted. Before ordering anything to eat or drink he said to the landlord, 'Is there a barber in the village who can give me a shave?' The landlord said there was and sent for him. The stranger told this barber, 'Take off my beard, but be careful, I have a sensitive skin! I'll pay you four thalers if you don't cut my face. But if you cut me I'll kill you! You wouldn't be the first!'

The barber was scared, for the stranger's scowl told him that he wasn't pretending and his sharp dagger lay on the table, so he ran off and sent along the journeyman. The soldier repeated his order. When the journeyman heard the conditions he too ran off and sent along the apprentice. The apprentice was dazzled by the money and thought, 'I'll risk it! If I manage it and don't cut him, for four thalers I can buy a new coat at the fair, and a lancet. If I don't, I know what I'll do!' And so he shaved his customer. His customer sat very still, he didn't know what mortal danger he was in, and the bold apprentice coolly drew the razor over his face and around his nose as if there was only threepence at stake or a dab of tinder or blotting-paper to staunch any cut he might make, rather than four thalers and his life, and he took off his beard nicely without cutting him or drawing blood, and when he had finished he thought: Thank God for that!

The man got up, looked at himself in the mirror and dried his face, and then he gave the lad the four thalers and said to him, 'Now tell me, young fellow, who gave you the courage to shave me when your master and the journeyman ran away? For if you'd cut me I would have killed you!' The apprentice smiled, thanked him for the handsome payment and said, 'Oh no, sir, you wouldn't have killed me, for if you had twitched and I'd cut your face I would have been quicker than you, I'd have slit your throat and made my getaway!' When the stranger heard that and thought of the danger he had been in he suddenly turned pale with fear and gave the lad another thaler, and since then he has never again told a barber, 'If you cut me I'll kill you!'

A Curious Ghost Story

Last autumn a gentleman was travelling through Schliengen, a nice little place. And as he was walking up the hill to spare the horses he told a man from Grenzach the following story of what had happened to him.

Six months earlier this gentleman was on his way to Denmark, and late one evening he arrived in a village with a fine mansion on a hill outside, and he wanted to stay the night. But the innkeeper said he had no room, there was a hanging the next day and three hangmen were staying with him. So the gentleman replied, 'Then I'll ask up there in the big house. The owner, the governor or whoever he is, will take me in and find a spare bed for me.' The innkeeper said, 'There are plenty of fine beds with silk hangings up there all ready made up, and I'm in charge of the keys. But I wouldn't advise you to go there! Three months ago the lord and the lady and the young master went away on a long journey, and since then the mansion house has been haunted by ghosts. The steward and the servants had to leave, and all the others who have been to the house never went back a second time.' Our stranger smiled. For he was a plucky man who wasn't afraid of ghosts, and he said, 'I'll risk it!' Despite all the innkeeper's objections he had to hand over the key, and after the traveller had put together what was needed to pay a visit on ghosts he went to the mansion with his servant who was travelling with him.

Once inside he didn't undress or get ready for bed, but waited to see what happened. He put two lights to burn on the table and a pair of loaded pistols next to them, and to pass away the time he picked up the Rhinelanders' Family Friend, bound in gold paper, which was hanging by red silk ribbon under the mirror in its frame on the wall, and looked at the nice pictures. For a long time nothing happened. But when midnight stirred in the church tower and the clock struck twelve, and a rainstorm was passing over the house and large drops were beating against the window, there were three loud knocks on the door and a ghastly apparition with black squinting eyes, a nose half a yard long, gnashing teeth, a beard like a goat and hair all over its body came into the room and said in a horrible growl: 'I am the lord Mephistopheles. Welcome to my palace! Have you said your goodbyes to your wife and children?' The visitor felt a cold shiver run up from his big toes over his back and up under his nightcap, and his poor servant was in a worse state still. But when this Mephistopheles came towards him, scowling dreadfully and stepping high as if he was crossing a floor of flames, the unfortunate gentleman thought: in God's name, this is the test! And he stood up boldly and pointed his pistol at the monster and said, 'Halt, or I'll shoot!' Not every ghost can be stopped like that, for even if you pull the trigger it doesn't go off, or the bullet flies back and hits you instead of the target. But Mephistopheles raised his first finger in warning, turned slowly on his heels and strode away just as he had come. Now when our traveller saw that this devil had respect for gunpowder, he thought, 'There's no danger now!', picked up a light in his free hand and followed the ghost cautiously along the passage; and his servant who was standing behind him ran for all he was worth out of this blessed place and down to the village, thinking he'd sooner spend the night with the hangmen than with spooks.

But suddenly in the passage the ghost disappeared from under the eyes of its plucky pursuer just as if it had gone through the floor. And when the gentleman went on another few paces to see where it had gone, all at once there was no floor under his feet and he fell down through a hole towards a flaming fire, and he himself thought he was on the way to hell. But after dropping about ten feet he found himself lying unharmed on a heap of hay in a cellar. And six weird fellows were standing around the fire, that Mephistopheles with them. All sorts of strange implements were piled up around them, and two tables stood heaped with shining thalers, each one more lovely than the other.

Now the stranger knew what was going on. For this was a secret band of forgers, all with blood running in their veins. They had taken advantage of the owner's absence and set up their mint in his mansion, and some of them were probably servants of the house who knew their way about; and to make sure they were not disturbed and discovered they wailed like ghosts, and anyone who came to the house was so frightened he never came back to take a second look. Yet the plucky traveller now had cause to regret his lack of prudence in not listening to the innkeeper's warnings. For he was pushed through a narrow opening into a small dark room and could hear them deciding his fate: 'The best thing is to kill him!' said one. But another said, 'First we must question him, find out who he is and where he's from.' When they then learnt he was a man of consequence and on his way to Copenhagen to see the king they looked at each other wide-eyed. And when he was back in the dark storeroom they said, 'This is a bad business. For if he's missed and they find out from the innkeeper that he came here and didn't leave, the hussars will come overnight and fetch us out, and there's plenty of hemp in the fields this year, so hangmen's nooses come cheap.' So they told their prisoner they would let him go if he swore an oath not to betray them, threatening they would have him watched in Copenhagen. And he had to tell them on oath where he lived. He told them, 'Next to the Green Man, on the left in the big house with green shutters.' Then they poured him some Burgundy wine and he watched them coining their thalers until it was light.

When the morning light shone down through the gratings, and they heard the sound of whips on the road and the cowherd blowing his horn, the traveller took leave of his night-time companions, thanked them for having him and went gaily back to the inn, quite forgetting that he had left his watch and pipe and the pistols behind in the mansion. The innkeeper said, 'Thank God you're back, I didn't get a wink of sleep! How did you get on?' But the traveller thought, an oath is an oath, and you mustn't take God's name in vain to save your life. So he said nothing, and as the bell was ringing and the wretched malefactor was being led out everyone ran off to watch. He said nothing in Copenhagen either, and almost forgot the incident himself.

A few weeks later, however, he received a parcel by the post, and in it were a pair of expensive new pistols inlaid with silver, a new gold watch set with diamonds, a Turkish pipe with a gold chain and a silk tobacco-pouch embroidered with gold, and in the pouch was a note. It said, 'We are sending you this to make up for the fright we gave you and to thank you for keeping quiet. It's all over now, and you can tell anyone you like.' So the traveller told the man from Grenzach, and it was that same gold watch that he took out at the top of the hill to check that the clock at Hertingen was striking noon on time, and later on in the Stork in Basel a French general offered him seventy-five new doubloons for it. But he wouldn't part with it.

The Hussar in Neisse

When at the beginning of the French Revolution the Prussians were at war with the French and advancing through the province of Champagne they didn't think that one day the tables might be turned and that in 1806 the French would be in Prussia repaying the uninvited visit. For they didn't all behave in the enemy land as good soldiers should. A swarthy Prussian hussar, for instance, a nasty type, forced his way into a peaceful civilian's home and took all his money and much else of value besides. In the end he even took the fine bed with its brand new covers, and he maltreated the man and his wife. An eight-year-old boy fell on his knees, imploring him to give them back his parents' bed, if nothing else. The pitiless hussar pushed him away. The daughter ran after him, caught hold of him by the tunic, and she too was pleading for mercy. He picked her up and threw her into the well in the yard and went off with his loot. Some time later he was discharged and settled in the town of Neisse in Silesia, and thought no more of what he had done, much water had flowed under the bridge since then.

But do you know what happened in 1806? The French entered Neisse; and one evening a young sergeant was quartered on a good woman who treated him well. The sergeant too was a decent fellow and behaved well and seemed to be happy. The next morning he didn't come down for breakfast. The woman thought he must be still asleep and kept his coffee warm. But when he still didn't appear she went up to his room, opened the door quietly and peeped in to see if anything was wrong.

The young man was awake, sitting up in bed, wringing his hands and sighing as if something terrible had happened or he was homesick or something of the sort, and he didn't notice her. But she went quietly up to him and asked, 'What has happened, sergeant, why are you so sad?' He looked at her with tears in his eyes and said the covers on this bed in which he had slept that night had once, eighteen years before, belonged to his parents in Champagne, they had lost everything in the looting and so were reduced to poverty, and now it had all come back to his mind and filled his heart with grief. For he was the son of the man in Champagne and remembered the covers still, and the initials his mother had embroidered on them in red were still there. The good woman was dismayed and told him she had bought the bedding from a swarthy hussar who lived here in Neisse, it was none of her doing. Now the Frenchman got up and had her take him to the hussar's house, and he recognized him.

'Do you remember,' he said to the hussar, 'how eighteen years ago in Champagne you robbed an innocent man of all his belongings and even took his bed from his house and showed no mercy when an eight-year-old boy pleaded with you to spare them? And my sister too?' At first the wretch tried to excuse himself: in war unfortunate things happen, and if you don't take something someone else will, so why not look after number one? But when he saw that the sergeant was the boy whose parents he had looted and maltreated, and when he reminded him of his sister, his bad conscience and his fear robbed him of speech and he fell trembling to his knees and could say only, 'Forgive me!' Yet he was thinking, this won't do much good!

Perhaps you too, good reader, are thinking, now the Frenchman will give the hussar a good thrashing, and you're looking forward to it? But that didn't happen, nor could it! For if someone's heart is broken with grief he is in no mood for vengeance, vengeance seems small and contemptible to him.

Rather he thinks, 'We are in God's hands', and has no desire to repay evil with evil. And that's how the Frenchman felt, and he said, 'You were cruel to me, I forgive you that. You were cruel to my parents and reduced them to poverty, they will forgive you that. You threw my sister into the well and she never got out again, may God forgive you that!' Saying this he left without laying a hand on the hussar, and he felt happier again. But the hussar afterwards felt as if he had stood at the Last Judgement and been found wanting. From that moment on he knew no peace of mind, and we are told he died about three months later.

Remember: When in a foreign land you should do nothing you would not have known by those back home.

Remember: Certain crimes are never forgotten, however much water flows under the bridge.

One Word Leads to Another

A rich man in Swabia sent his son to Paris to learn French and a few manners. After a year or more his father's farmhand came to see him. The son was greatly surprised and cried out joyfully, 'Hans, whatever are you doing here? How are things at home, what's the news?'

'Nothing much, Mr William, though your fine raven copped it two weeks ago, the one the gamekeeper gave you.'

'Oh, the poor bird,' replied Mr William. 'What happened to it?'

'Well, you see, he ate too much carrion when our fine horses died one after the other. I said he would.'

'What! My father's four fine greys are dead?' Mr William asked. 'How did that happen?'

'Well, you see, they were worked too hard hauling water when the house and the barns burned down, and it did no good.'

'Oh no!' exclaimed Mr William, horrified. 'Our house burnt down? When was that?'

'Well, you see, nobody thought of a fire when your father lay in his coffin. He was buried at night with torches. A small spark soon spreads.'

'That's terrible news!' exclaimed Mr William in his distress. 'My father dead? And how is my sister?'

'Well, you see, your late father died of grief when the young Miss had a child and no father for it. It's a boy.

'There's nothing much else to tell,' he added.

Moses Mendelssohn

Moses Mendelssohn was of the Jewish faith and worked for a merchant who didn't actually invent the wheel, yet was god-fearing and wise and therefore respected and liked by the most eminent and learned men.* And that is only right. For you mustn't judge a man by the length of his hair. The said Moses Mendelssohn was content with his lot, as this story shows. For one day a friend came to him while he was sweating over some tricky accounts and said to him, 'It's a real shame, my good Moses, it's a scandal that a clever fellow like you has to work for a man who's not fit to hold a candle to him! After all, you have as much brain in your little finger as he has in his whole fat body!' That would have rankled with anyone else, he would have thrown pen and inkpot into the fire with a few curses after them and given his notice on the spot. But the sensible Mendelssohn did not reach for the inkpot, he stuck his pen behind his ear, looked calmly at his friend and said this: 'Things are well as they are and the work of wise providence. For my master can profit from my services and I have a livelihood. If I were the master and he my clerk I would have no use for him.'

A Dear Head and a Cheap One

When the last King of Poland* was still on the throne there was a rebellion against him, one of several. One of the rebels, a Polish prince, was rash enough to set a price of twenty thousand guilders on the king's head. Indeed he had the impudence to inform the king himself of this in writing, to dishearten or frighten him. But the king replied quite coolly, 'I have received and read your letter. I am pleased that you still place a value on my head. For I can assure you I wouldn't give a brass farthing for yours.'

Expensive Eggs

Some time ago a foreign prince was travelling through France when his stomach began to feel a little hollow, so he stopped at a common inn where such custom is normally never seen, and ordered three boiled eggs. When he had eaten the landlord demanded three hundred livres. The prince asked if eggs were in such short supply there. The landlord smiled and said, 'No, not eggs, but grand gentlemen who can pay that much for them!' The prince smiled too and paid up, and that was good. But when the King of France at that time heard of this (it was told him as a joke) he was not at all pleased that an innkeeper in his land should dare to overcharge so shamelessly, and he told the prince, 'When you pass that inn on your way home you will see that justice reigns in my land!' And when the prince passed the inn on his journey home the signboard had gone, the doors and windows were bricked up, and that was good too.

The Three Thieves

You, good reader, are warned not to think that everything that happens in this story is true. Yet it is told in a fine book, and in verses too!*

From an early age Harry and Freddy Tinder followed in the trade of their father, who had already got entangled with a rope-maker's daughter called Noose at the gallows in Auerbach; and a schoolfriend, Carrot-Top Jack, joined them, and he was the youngest. But they didn't murder or attack people, they just paid night calls on hen-houses, and if they had the chance on kitchens, cellars and storerooms too, maybe the occasional money box, and at markets no one bought cheaper than they did. But when there was nothing around to steal they practised all sorts of tasks and tricks together so as to progress in their craft. Once, when they were in the forest, Harry spotted a bird sitting on its nest high up in a tree, guessed it must have eggs, and asked the other two: 'Who can take the eggs from that bird's-nest up there without the bird noticing?' Freddy climbed aloft like a cat, crept quietly up to the nest, poked a hole through the bottom, let the eggs drop through into his hand one after the other, made good the nest with moss, and came down with the eggs. 'Now, who can put the eggs back under the bird', said Freddy, 'without the bird noticing?' So now Harry climbed up the tree, but Freddy climbed up after him, and as Harry was slowly pushing the eggs back under the bird without the bird noticing Freddy slowly pulled down Harry's trousers without Harry noticing. They had a good laugh, and the other two said, 'Freddy wins!' But Carrot-Top Jack said, 'I see I can't keep up with you two, and if we ever get detained at someone else's pleasure and the devil catches up on us I shan't be scared for you, but for myself I will!' So he left them and became an honest man again, and went back to a quiet life of work at home with his wife.

In the autumn, not long after the other two had stolen a pony at the horse fair, they called on Jack to ask how he was doing; for they had heard that he had killed a pig and intended to keep an eye open for it. It was hanging on the wall in the larder. When they had left Jack said to his wife, 'I'll take the porker into the kitchen and hide it under the trough, otherwise it will be gone by the morning!' That night the thieves came back and made a hole in the wall as quietly as they could, but their prize was no longer there. Jack heard something, got up and walked round outside the house to check. Harry sneaked round the other side of the house, in through the door and up to the bed where Jack's wife lay, imitated her husband's voice and said, 'Wife, the pig has gone from the larder!' She said, 'Don't be silly! You put it under the trough in the kitchen!' 'Of course!' said Harry, 'I'm still half asleep,' and went and took the pig and carried it off safely. But he couldn't find his brother in the dark and reckoned that he would join him in the forest at the spot they'd arranged. And when Jack came back into the house and went to check on the pig he cried, 'Wife, those scallywags have taken it after all!' Yet he didn't admit defeat so easily, he went after the thieves, and when he caught up with Harry (he was already some way from the house) and saw that he was on his own, he promptly imitated Freddy's voice and said, 'Brother, let me carry the porker now, you'll be getting tired.' Harry thought it was his brother and gave him the pig and said he would go on ahead into the forest and make a fire. But Jack turned round behind his back and said to himself, 'Now you're mine again, you lovely little piggy!' and carried the pig home. Meanwhile Freddy wandered around in the dark until he saw the fire in the forest and found his brother and said, 'Where's the pig then, Harry?' Harry said, 'Don't you have it then, Freddy?' Now they looked at each other wide-eyed and could have done without the fire of beech chips crackling away for the feast in the night.

By now an even finer fire was roaring away back home in Jack's kitchen. For as soon as he got back to the house the pig was cut up and put to cook in a pot over the fire. You see, Jack said, 'Wife, I'm hungry, and if we don't eat it quickly those rogues will get it after all.' Then he slumped down in a corner and dozed off, and while his wife was stirring the meat with an iron fork he groaned in his sleep and she looked over at him, and at that moment a sharp stick came slowly down the chimney and speared the best piece in the pot and lifted it up and away. And when he made ever more frightened whimpers in his sleep and his wife eyed him with ever greater concern the stick appeared a second and then a third time. And when Jack's wife woke him, 'We can serve up now!' she said, the pot was empty, and now they too could have done without their fire crackling away for the feast in the night. But as they were about to go to bed hungry and were thinking, 'If the devil means to have the pig there's nothing we can do about it,' the thieves came down from the roof and through the hole in the wall into the larder and from there into the room, and they brought back what they had spirited away.

Now they really made a party of it! They ate and drank, joked and laughed as if they knew it was for the last time, and enjoyed themselves until the moon in its last quarter was going down over the house and the cocks in the village were crowing for the second time and the butcher's dog was barking in the distance. For the constables were on the trail, and just as Carrot-Top Jack's wife was saying, 'Now we really must get to bed!', the constables came about the stolen pony and took Harry and Freddy Tinder off to jail to be put away behind lock and key.

The Emperor Napoleon and the Fruit Woman in Brienne

The great Emperor Napoleon spent his youth as a cadet in the military school at Brienne. Do you wonder what kind of a pupil he was? You can tell that from the way he led his armies into war and from his other actions. Like other youngsters he was fond of fruit, and a certain woman who sold fruit in Brienne earned a good few pennies from him. When he had no money she gave him credit. When he had the money he paid her. But when he left the school as a well-trained soldier to put what he had learnt into practice he owed her a few thalers. You see, as she brought him a plate of juicy peaches or sweet grapes for the last time he said, 'Young lady, I have to leave now and I can't pay you. But you won't be forgotten.' But the fruit woman said, 'Just you go and don't let it worry you, young sir. May God keep you in good health and bring you happiness!'

But in the career the young soldier was about to begin such a thing can be forgotten even by the best memory in the world, until in the end a grateful heart gives it a jog. Soon Napoleon was made a general and conquered Italy. Napoleon went to Egypt where the children of Israel once made bricks and he fought a battle near Nazareth* where the Blessed Virgin lived eighteen hundred years ago. Napoleon sailed straight back to France over a sea swarming with enemy ships, arrived in Paris and became First Consul. Napoleon restored peace and law and order to his troubled country and became French Emperor, and still the good fruitseller in Brienne had nothing except his word, 'You won't be forgotten!' But that word was worth as much as cash in hand, and more. For one day when the Emperor was expected in Brienne, though nobody knew it he was already there, and he must have been moved as he thought of the past times and the present and how in so short a space of time God had led him safely through so many dangers and placed him on the new imperial throne – and all at once he stopped in his tracks and put his hand to his brow like someone remembering something, and after a few moments he spoke the fruit woman's name and found out where she lived, in a house that was almost a ruin, and he went there with just one trusty companion. A narrow doorway led him into a small but tidy room where the woman with her two children was kneeling at the fire preparing a frugal supper.

'Do you have any fresh fruit?' asked the Emperor. 'Indeed I do,' replied the woman, 'the melons are ripe,' and she fetched one. She was putting a few more sticks on the fire and the two strangers were eating the melon when one of them asked, 'Do you know the Emperor who is supposed to be here today?' 'He isn't here yet,' the woman replied. 'He's still on his way. Do I know him, indeed! He bought many a dish or basket of fruit from me when he was at school here.' 'And did he pay for everything?' 'Of course he did, he paid all right.' Then the stranger said to her, 'Woman, either you are not telling the truth or you must have a bad memory. For one thing, you don't know the Emperor. For I'm the Emperor! Furthermore, I didn't pay for everything

as you say, rather I think I owe you something like two thalers!' And at this point his companion counted out 1,200 francs on the table, principal and interest. Now that the woman recognized the Emperor and heard the gold coins ring on the table she fell at his feet and was beyond herself with astonishment and joy and gratitude, and her children looked at each other and didn't know what to say. Afterwards the Emperor ordered the house to be torn down and a new one to be built for her on the same spot. 'I shall stay in this house,' he said, 'whenever I come to Brienne and it shall be called after me.' And he promised the woman that he would look after her children.

He has in fact already made honourable provision for her daughter, and her son is being educated at the Emperor's expense at the same school from which the great hero himself started out.

The Bombardment of Copenhagen

In the whole dangerous time from 1789 on, when one country after another was drawn into revolution or bloody war, Denmark remained at peace, thanks partly to its position and partly to the wisdom of its government. It sided with no one and harmed nobody, desiring only the welfare of its subjects, and was therefore respected by all the powers. When, however, in 1807 the English saw that Russia and Prussia had deserted them and made peace with the enemy,* and that the French held all the harbours and strong points on the Baltic and matters would be worse if they moved into Denmark, they said nothing, but put a fleet to sea, and no one knew where it was heading. Then, when the fleet stood in the sound off the Danish coast and outside the Danish capital city and royal residence of Copenhagen, and all was peaceful and quiet, the English sent this message to Copenhagen: 'Since we are such good friends kindly hand over your fleet until the end of the war so that it doesn't fall into the hands of the enemy, and the fort with it. For we would be terribly sorry to have to shoot the town down over your heads!' It was just as if a townsman or a farmer who has a quarrel at law with a neighbour were to take his men with him and go in to another neighbour in bed at night and say, 'Neighbour, since I am fighting a case against that fellow you must give me your horse to keep until it is settled, so that he can't use it to ride to the lawyers – if you don't I'll burn your house down! And you must let me stand with my men in your cornfield beside the road so that if he tries to go to court on his own horse we can stop him.' That neighbour would say: 'You leave my house out of it! What's your quarrel to do with me?' And that's what the Danes said.

When the English said, 'Will you oblige us or won't you?' and the Danes said, 'No, we won't!', they put landing parties ashore and moved in towards the town, erected batteries and set up cannons in them, and told the Danes they had until 2 September after the peace of Tilsit. But the people of Copenhagen and the whole Danish nation said it was high-handed and quite outrageous and the sea could never wash out the shame of giving in to threats and agreeing to unjust demands. Definitely not!

So began the terrible punishment that fate had decreed for that unfortunate city. Copenhagen was bombarded by seventy-two mortars and heavy cannon without a pause from seven o'clock in the evening throughout the night for twelve hours. A devil by the name of Congreve* was part of it, he had invented a new weapon of destruction, the so-called fire-rockets. They were, roughly speaking, tubes filled with inflammable material and with a short arrow fixed to their front end. When the rocket was fired it set light to the material inside, and when it hit something in which the arrow could take hold it stuck there, often in places that couldn't be reached, and set fire to everything around that would burn. These fire-rockets too rained on Copenhagen all night long. At that time Copenhagen had 4,000 houses, 85,965 inhabitants, 22 churches, 4 royal palaces, 22 hospitals, and 30 poorhouses, it was a busy trading centre and had many factories. You can imagine how many fine roof-timbers were shot to pieces during that awful night, how many mothers' hearts and minds were paralysed by fear, how many wounds bled, and how the prayers and cries of despair mingled with the alarm bells and the thunder of the cannon.

When dawn broke on 3 September the shooting stopped; and the English asked if they would give in. The commandant of Copenhagen said, 'No!' So at four in the afternoon the bombardment began again, lasting until noon on 4 September with no let-up or mercy given. And as the commandant still wouldn't say yes, the firing resumed that evening and went on through the night until noon on the 5th. More than 300 fine houses had been burnt to cinders; whole church towers had collapsed and flames were still raging everywhere. More than 800 townspeople had been killed, and many badly wounded. All Copenhagen was in flames, or a heap of rubble, it looked like a field hospital or a battlefield.

Finally on 7 September the commandant of Copenhagen saw that all was lost and capitulated, and the Crown Prince didn't even thank him for it. Immediately the English took possession of the whole Danish fleet and sailed it away: eighteen ships of the line, fifteen frigates and a greater number of smaller ships, all except for one frigate that the King of England had given to the King of Denmark when they were still friends. That one they left. But the King of Denmark sent it to join the others, he didn't want any mementoes. The English let all hell loose on land and water, for soldiers know not what they do, they only think we wouldn't be fighting them if they didn't deserve it. Luckily they didn't stay long. They embarked again on 19 October and sailed away on the 21st with the Danish fleet and their booty. That fellow Congreve drowned on this trip and never saw his family again. The Danes then joined the French side, and the Emperor Napoleon refused to make peace with the English until they returned the ships and paid Copenhagen compensation.

There we have the fate of Denmark, and the friends of the English say they didn't mean any harm. But others say no greater harm could have been done, and the Danes see it that way too.

The Strange Fortunes of a Young Englishman

One day a young Englishman was on the mail coach on his first journey to the great city of London, where among all its inhabitants he knew only his brother-in-law whom he was going to visit, and his sister, that man's wife. He was alone on the coach too, but for the conductor (that's the person in charge of the coach and responsible for the letters and packets at each stage); and at that time these two fellow travellers had no thought for where they would next meet.

The coach didn't arrive in London until the dead of night. The young fellow couldn't stay the night in the posthouse because the postmaster there was a distinguished man who didn't let rooms, and he had as much chance of finding his brother-in-law's house in the huge city in the dark as of finding a needle in a haystack. So the conductor said to him, 'Come along with me, young man! I don't live here either, but when I'm in London I stay at my cousin's in a room with two beds in it. She will put you up all right, and tomorrow you can start looking for better lodgings at your brother-in-law's.' The young man did not have to be asked twice. At the cousin's house they drank a jug of English beer and had a bite of sausage and then went to bed.

In the night the young man needed to go outside. Now he was in an even worse fix than before. For he could no more hope to find his way in the small house where he was lodging than in the great city a few hours before. But luckily the conductor woke up too and told him where to go, left, then right, then left again. 'The door is locked,' he added, 'and we've lost the key. But take my big knife from my overcoat pocket and poke it between the door and the post and the catch inside will spring open. Just listen and you'll find it. You'll hear the sound of the Thames. And put something on, it's a cold night!' In his haste the young man picked up the conductor's jacket in the dark instead of his own, put it on, and found his destination all right. For it didn't bother him that he turned one of the corners too soon and bumped his nose so that he bled dreadfully on account of the strong beer he had drunk. But the loss of blood and the cold made him come over faint and he fell asleep.

The conductor lay in bed and waited and waited, he couldn't understand where the other fellow was all this time, until he heard a noise in the street and thought, half asleep, 'The poor devil's gone out through the front door into the lane and been pressed!' You see, when the English need crews for their ships, strong men are sent to roam the streets unannounced and they go into the common taverns and the houses of ill repute, and if anyone suitable falls into their hands they don't stop to ask him, 'Who might you be, my young fellow?' or 'What's your name, sir?', but make short work of it and drag him off willy nilly to the fleet, and God help him! Those taken on these nocturnal manhunts are said to be pressed into service; and so it was that our conductor thought, 'He must have been pressed!' In his alarm he sprang out of bed, threw his coat around him and rushed into the street to try to save the poor fellow. But when he followed the sounds down one street and into the next he himself fell into the hands of the press-gang and was dragged off – unwillingly – on to a ship, and the next day he was far away. He was gone.

Later the young man out the back came to, hurried back into bed just as he was without noticing that his room-mate wasn't there, and slept well into the next day. Meanwhile at eight o'clock the conductor was expected at the posthouse, and when time passed and there was no sign of him they sent someone to chase him up. He found, not the conductor, but a man lying in bed with blood on his clothes, a large knife on the corridor floor, blood leading to the privy, and the Thames flowing underneath. So the bloodstained stranger was suspected of murdering the conductor and throwing his body into the river. He was taken away to be questioned, and they searched him and found in the pocket of the jacket he was still wearing a leather purse with the conductor's easily identifiable silver signet ring fastened to its strings, and the unfortunate young fellow was done for. He gave the name of his brother-in-law – nobody knew him; and his sister's – nobody had heard of her. He told the whole story as far as he knew it. But the judges said, 'That's all eyewash! You shall be hanged!' No sooner said than done, that very same afternoon, according to English law and custom. You see, since London is full of villains the English custom is to make short work of a hanging, and few take much notice, it's such a common sight. The criminals, as many as there are at any one time, are loaded on to a cart and driven to the foot of the gallows. They fasten the rope to the hook up above, pull the cart away from underneath and leave the beauties to dangle, without bothering to look back. In England hanging is not such a great disgrace as here, it brings only death. That's because later the criminal's nearest and dearest come and pull down on his legs and make sure he's properly strangled.

But no one rendered this sad service of love and friendship for our stranger in town, and it was evening before a young husband and wife out walking arm in arm happened to come to the place of execution and looked up at the gallows as they passed by. With a cry of horror the woman fell into her husband's arms. 'Lord save us, that's our brother!' They were even more appalled when the hanged man, recognizing his sister's voice, opened his eyes and rolled them horribly in their sockets. He was still alive, you see, and the couple passing by were his sister and brother-in-law. Yet this brother-in-law was made of stern stuff and kept his head, and was quietly thinking how he might save him. It was an out-of-the-way place, everyone had moved off, and he managed with some money and a few well-phrased words to engage a couple of plucky and trusty lads who, as cool as you please, fetched down the hanged man as if they had every right to do it; and nobody challenged them as they carried him to the brother-in-law's house and safely indoors. There he was brought round in a few hours. He had a little fever, but to his sister's relief soon got quite well again under her tender care. But one evening his brother-in-law said to him, 'Brother! You can't stay here in this country now. You could be hanged again if they catch you, and me with you. And in any case you have worn a necklace round your neck that brought no honour to you or your family. You must go to America. I'll provide for you there.'

The young man saw that made sense, left as soon as he could on a trusty ship and eighty days later arrived safely in Philadelphia harbour. But when, sad at heart, he stepped ashore in that totally strange land, thinking, 'If only God would let me meet just one person who knows me' – lo and behold there, dressed as a poor sailor, was the conductor! Normally it's a great joy to meet someone you know so unexpectedly and so far from home, but in this case the greeting was by no means a warm one. For when the conductor saw who it was he approached with raised fist. 'Where the devil have you sprung from, you damned fly-by-night?' he said. 'Do you know I was press-ganged because of you?' And the Englishman said, 'Well I'll be damned! You accursed will-o'-the-wisp. Do you know I was hanged on your

account?' Yet after that they went together into the Three Crowns in Philadelphia and told each other how fate had treated them. And afterwards the young Englishman did well in a trading house and did not rest till he had bought his friend's discharge and was able to send him back to London again. He himself became rich in America and now lives in the town of Washington, at number 42 in the newest part of Merchants' Street.

Innocence is Hanged

The following unhappy incident took place in Spessart.

Some boys watched over their parents' or masters' cattle on a hillside under the forest. They played all sorts of games to pass the time away, and as such youngsters often do they pretended to be grown-ups about grown-up affairs. One day one of them said, 'I'll be the thief!' 'And I'll be the chief magistrate,' said the second. 'You be the bailiffs,' he said to two others, 'And you're the hangman,' to the one who was left. All right! The thief stole a knife from one of his mates and ran off. The theft was reported to the chief magistrate. The bailiffs combed the area, caught the thief in a hollow tree and brought him in. The magistrate sentenced him to death. Meanwhile a shot sounded in the wood and dogs began barking. The boys took no notice. The hangman put a rope round the criminal's neck and recklessly, stupid and ignorant as he was, strung him up from the branch of a tree so that his feet couldn't reach the ground, thinking he'd be all right if it was only for a moment or two. Suddenly there was a rustling in the dry leaves in the wood, a cracking and crashing in the thick undergrowth, and a wild boar, black and shaggy with gleaming tusks, broke cover and ran across the place of execution. The young cowherds, who had felt all along that perhaps it wasn't quite right to make a game of such a grave and ticklish business, thought it was the devil himself, God save us all from him, they took fright and fled, and one of them ran down to the village to say what had happened. But when the men arrived to free the boy from the gallows he was already strangled and dead. That should be a warning to others! The magistrate and the bailiffs were put into jail for three weeks, the hangman for six. It turned out that the black boar wasn't the devil after all. For it was killed by the huntsmen and taken to the forester's house. But then we know Satan is still alive and active.

A Bad Bargain

In the great city of London and round about it there are an extraordinary number of silly fools who take a childish delight in other people's money or fob watches or precious rings and don't rest until they have them for themselves. Sometimes they get them by cunning and trickery, but more often by fearless assault, sometimes in broad daylight on the open road. Some of them do well, others don't. The London jailors and executioners can tell a few tales about that! One day, however, a strange thing happened to a certain rich and distinguished man. The King and many other great lords and their ladies were gathered on a lovely summer's day in a royal park where the winding paths led to a wood in the distance. Crowds of other people were there too, they didn't think their journey or their time wasted if they could see that their beloved King and his family were happy and well. There was food and drink, music and dancing. There were walks to be taken in pairs or alone along the inviting paths and between scented rose bushes. A man, well-dressed so that he appeared to be one of the company, took up his stand with a pistol under his coat by a tree at a secluded spot where the park bordered on the wood, waiting for someone to come his way. And someone did come, a gentleman with a ring sparkling on his finger, a tinkling watch chain, diamonds in his buckles, and a ribbon and a star on his breast. He was strolling in the cool shade and thinking of nothing in particular. And while he was thinking of nothing in particular the fellow behind the tree stepped out, bowed low, pulled his pistol from under his coat, pointed it at the gentleman's breast and asked him politely to keep quiet, no one need know about their conversation! You can't help feeling uneasy when a pistol is aimed at you, you can never be sure what's in it! The gentleman very sensibly thought: better your money than your life, better lose a ring than a finger! and he promised to keep quiet.

'Now, Your Honour,' said this fellow, 'would you part with your two gold watches for a good price? Our schoolmaster adjusts the clock every day, so we can never be sure of the right time, and you can't see the figures on the sundial.' The gentleman had no choice, he was obliged to sell his watches to the scoundrel for a few pence, hardly the price of a glass of wine. In this way the rascal bought his ring and his buckles and the decorations off his breast, one after another and each for a paltry sum, with the pistol in his left hand all the time. When at last the gentleman thought, now he'll let me go, thank God!, the rogue began again.

'Your Honour, since we do business so easily, why don't you buy some of my things from me?' The gentleman thought, I must grin and bear it, that's the expression, and said, 'Show me what you have!' The fellow took a collection of trinkets from his pocket, things he had bought at a tuppenny stall or filched from somewhere, and the gentleman had to buy them all from him, one after the other, none of them cheap. Eventually the rogue had nothing left but the pistol, but seeing that the gentleman still had a couple of lovely doubloons in his green silk purse he said, 'Sir, won't you buy this pistol of mine with what's left in your purse? It's made by the best gunmaker in London and it's worth two doubloons of anyone's money!' The gentleman was surprised. 'This robber's an idiot!' he thought, and bought the

pistol. When he had bought it from the robber he turned the tables on him and said: 'Hands up, my fine friend, and do as I tell you, keep walking in front of me or I'll blow your brains out!' But the rogue darted off into the wood. 'Go ahead and shoot, Your Excellency,' he said, 'it's not loaded!' The gentleman pulled the trigger, and in fact it didn't go off. He pushed the ramrod into the barrel, there was no trace of powder. By now the thief was well away into the wood; and the distinguished Englishman walked back, red in the face at being frightened by an empty threat, and he had something to think about now.

A Profitable Game of Riddles

Eleven people were on a boat going down the Rhine from Basel, and a Jew who was making for Chalampé was allowed to travel with them and sit in a corner so long as he behaved himself and tipped the boatman eighteen kreuzers. The Jew's purse jingled right enough when he shook it, but it contained only one twelve-kreuzer piece; its companion was a brass button. Nevertheless he accepted the offer gratefully. For he thought, 'There'll be something to be made underway, many have got rich on the Rhine before now.'

To begin with, on leaving the Tankard Inn, they chattered and joked a great deal, and the Jew, who didn't take off his cloth pack but kept it firmly on his shoulder, sat there in his corner and had to put up with a great deal: it's a wrong sometimes done to his kind. But when they were well past Öhningen and Cobbler's Island, past Märkt and the cliff at Istein and St Vitus's Chapel, one by one they all fell quiet and yawned and gazed down the length of the Rhine, until one of them broke the silence. 'You, Moses,' he said, 'Don't you know some way of whiling away our time? Your forefathers must have thought up all sorts of things in the wilderness.'

'Now,' thought the Jew, 'here's a chance to feather my nest,' and he suggested they take turns to ask riddles, and he would join in if they would allow him. All those who couldn't solve a riddle were to give the one who set it a twelve-kreuzer piece, a good answer would earn the same sum. The whole company was happy with that, and hoping they would be amused by the Jew's stupidity, or his clever idea, they each asked merrily whatever came into his head. The first, for example, asked: 'How many soft-boiled eggs could the giant Goliath eat on an empty stomach?' They all said no one could possibly guess that and paid out twelve kreuzers each. But the Jew said, 'Just one, for when you've eaten one egg your stomach is no longer empty!' He had won the twelve kreuzers.

The next one thought, 'You wait, Jew, I'll test you on the New Testament, that way I won't lose my twelve kreuzers!' 'Why did the apostle Paul write the Second Epistle to the Corinthians?' The Jew said, 'He can't have been with them, if he had he could have spoken to them.' That was another twelve kreuzers.

When the third man saw that the Jew was well versed in the Bible he started on a different tack: 'Who draws out his work as long as he can but still finishes it on time?' The Jew said, 'The ropemaker who is good at his job.'

The fourth one asked: 'Who gets paid for pulling wool over people's eyes?' The Jew said, 'A wigmaker.'

Meanwhile they were approaching a village and one of them said, 'That's Bamlach.' Then the fifth asked: 'In which month do the people of Bamlach eat least?' The Jew said, 'In February, it has only twenty-eight days.'

The sixth said: 'There are two brothers born of the same mother, but only one of them is a distant relative of mine.' The Jew said, 'The distant relative lives some way away from you, the other brother lives nearby.'

A fish leapt out of the water, so the seventh asked: 'Which fishes have their eyes closest together?' The Jew said, 'The smallest.'

The eighth asked: 'How can you ride in the shade from Basel to Berne in the summer when the sun is shining ever so hot?' The Jew said, 'When there's no shade you get off and walk.'

The ninth riddle was: 'If someone is riding from Basel to Berne in winter and has forgotten his gloves, how can he see to it that he doesn't get frozen hands?' The Jew said, 'He can clench both hands and change them into fists.'

The tenth asked: 'Why does a cooper sneak unseen into his barrels?' The Jew said, 'Because barrels have no doors through which an honest man might enter.'

That left number eleven. He asked: 'How can five people share five eggs so that each of them gets one and one is still left in the bowl?' The Jew said, 'The last man takes the bowl with the egg in it, then he can leave it in the bowl as long as he likes.'

Now it was his turn, and he meant to make a good picking. With much bowing and scraping and a wily winning smile he asked: 'How can you cook two trout in three pans so that there is one trout in each pan?' No one could answer that, and all of them in turn gave the Israelite a twelve-kreuzer piece.

Your Family Friend would like to put this same question to all his readers, from Milan up to Copenhagen, and so make a nice pile, more than he gets from the Almanac which pays him little. For when the eleven of them demanded that the Jew earn his money and solve this riddle too, he turned doubtfully this way and that, shrugging his shoulders and rolling his eyes. Eventually he said, 'I'm only a poor Jew.' The others said, 'Spare us the build-up! Tell us the answer!' 'No offence meant,' was the reply, 'I am only a poor Jew, you know!' Finally, after much persuasion and assurances that if only he would give the answer they wouldn't take anything amiss, he put his hand in his pocket and took out one of the twelve-kreuzer pieces he had won, put it on the table in front of him and said, 'I don't know the answer either. So there's my twelve kreuzers!'

When the others heard that they gaped and said he had cheated. But since they had to laugh nevertheless and were rich and good-hearted men, and their companion, the Hebrew, had whiled away the time for them from Kleinkems to Chalampé, they let the matter stand, and the Jew left the boat with . . . Now then, which of you can work it out in your head! How much did the Jew take away, in guilders and kreuzers? He had twelve kreuzers and a brass button to start with. He won eleven twelve-kreuzer pieces solving the riddles, eleven times twelve kreuzers with his own riddle, paid back one of the coins, and gave an eighteen-kreuzer tip to the boatman.

The Recruit

In 1795 a fine well-built lad joined the Swabian Regiment as a recruit. The officer asked him how old he was. The recruit replied, 'Twenty-one. I was ill for a whole year, otherwise I'd be twenty-two.'

The Ropemaker's Reply

A horsethief in Donauwörth was hanged when his time came, and Your Family Friend has often wondered, 'Why does someone who's heading for the gallows or the jail one of these days need to steal a horse? Wouldn't he get there soon enough on foot?' This fellow from Donauwörth was one of those who thought the gallows wouldn't wait for him unless he was on horseback, and just as the horse fell into the hands of a stupid thief, the thief fell into the hands of a stupid hangman. You see, the hangman had put the necklace of hemp on him and pushed him off the rung of the ladder, but for some time he still rolled his eyes from one side to the other as if he were searching around in the crowd for another horse for himself. For many had come on horseback or on haycarts so as to have a better view. But when the crowd began to voice their disapproval and the incompetent hangman was at a loss what to do, eventually in his panic he threw himself at the dangling man, embraced him with both arms as if to bid him farewell and pulled with all his might so as to tighten the noose and strangle him. Now the rope broke and both of them fell to the ground together, and they might just as well never have climbed the scaffold. The criminal was still alive, and his lawyer later saved him. For he said, 'The miscreant stole only one horse, not two, therefore he has earned only one hanging,' and he added lots of letters and numbers in Latin as lawyers do. But the hangman loosed his anger on the ropemaker when he saw him that afternoon: 'Do you call that a rope?' he said. 'Someone should have strung you up with it!' The ropemaker had an answer to that: 'Nobody told me,' he said, 'it had to carry two scoundrels. It was strong enough for one, you or the horsethief!'

The Cure

For all their piles of shekels rich people sometimes still have to put up with all sorts of troubles and illnesses of which a poor man, thank God, knows nothing. For there are illnesses that don't lurk in the air but in full plates and glasses, in soft armchairs and silken beds. A certain rich citizen of Amsterdam could tell you a thing or two on that score! He would spend the whole morning sitting in his armchair, smoking if he wasn't too sluggish, or gazing out of the window, but at midday he ate like a horse, and sometimes his neighbours said, 'Is that the wind getting up outside or is it the neighbour snorting?' He ate and drank all afternoon too, something cold perhaps, and then something hot, not because he was hungry or fancied a particular dish but just to pass away the time till evening, so that you couldn't rightly say where his dinner finished and his supper began. After supper he went to bed as weary as if he'd been heaving stones or chopping logs all day long. Thus in time his body grew fat and as ungainly as a sack of corn. Neither eating nor sleeping gave him pleasure, and for some time, as quite often happens, he was neither very well nor very ill. But he would have told you he had 365 illnesses, a different one for each day of the year. Each and every doctor in Amsterdam was called upon to treat him. He swallowed whole fire-buckets full of mixtures, powders by the shovelful, and pills as big as ducks' eggs, and people joked and called him the apothecary's shelf on two legs. But all the treatments did him no good, for he didn't do as the doctors told him but said, 'Hang it all, what's the point of being rich if I have to live a dog's life and all the money in the world can't get a doctor to cure me?'

Eventually he heard of a doctor who lived a hundred hours' journey away: it was said he was so clever that his patients got well as soon as he looked at them and that Death slunk away as soon as he came on the scene. Our man pinned his hopes on this doctor and wrote to him of his complaints. This doctor quickly saw what he needed all right, not medicine, that is, but moderation and exercise, and said, 'You wait, I'll soon have you cured!' So he wrote him a letter as follows: 'My friend, you are in a bad way, but you can be helped if you do as I tell you. You have a nasty beast in your belly, a dragon with seven mouths. I must deal with this dragon myself, so you'll have to come here to me. But first of all you must not come by coach or on horse but on Shanks's pony, otherwise you will shake up the dragon and it will rip out your guts, biting right through seven intestines all at once. Second, you must not eat more than a plate of vegetables twice a day, with a sausage at midday and an egg in the evening and a bowl of broth with chives on top in the morning. Anything more than that will only make the dragon grow so that it will crush your liver, and then it won't be your tailor who takes your measurements, but the undertaker. That's my advice and if you don't heed it you won't live to hear the cuckoo next spring! It's up to you!' The very next morning after reading that, the patient had his boots waxed and set off as the doctor had ordered. On that first day he walked so slowly that a snail could have run ahead to announce his progress, and he ignored those who greeted him on his way and stamped on every tiny creature that was crawling on the ground. But already on the second and third mornings the birds seemed to be singing more sweetly than for many a year, and he thought the dew so fresh and the poppies in the fields so bright, and everyone he met seemed so nice, and he was too. And each morning when he left his lodging place the world was more beautiful and he strode on his way more easily and more cheerfully. On the eighteenth day he reached the doctor's town, and when he got up the next morning he felt so well he said, 'I couldn't have got better at a worse time, just when I have to see the doctor! I just wish my ears were ringing a bit or I had a touch of dropsy!' When he went in to see the doctor, the doctor took hold of his hand and said, 'Now then, start from the beginning again and tell me what's wrong with you.' He replied, 'Doctor, nothing is wrong with me, praise God, and I hope you are as well as I am.' The doctor said, 'I see a good spirit told you to take my advice. The dragon has gone. But its eggs are still inside you, and you must therefore go back home on foot, and when you get back you must saw lots of wood when no one's watching and eat only enough to satisfy your hunger so that the eggs don't hatch, and then you may live to a good old age.' And he smiled as he spoke. But the rich patient who had come so far said, 'Sir, you are a weird one, yet I think I take your meaning,' and after that he followed his advice and lived for eighty-seven years four months and ten days, a picture of health, and every New Year he sent the doctor twenty doubloons with his best wishes:

How Freddy Tinder and His Brother Played Another Trick on Carrot-Top Jack

When Harry and Freddy Tinder were out of jail again Harry said to his brother, 'Freddy, let's call in on Carrot-Top Jack, otherwise he'll think we were put away between cold damp walls for ever!' 'We'll play a trick on him,' said Freddy to Harry, 'and see if he knows it's us!' So it was that Jack got an anonymous note: 'Carrot-Top Jack, watch out tonight! Two thieves have made a bet that one of them will steal the sheet from under your wife and you won't be able to stop them.' Jack said, 'Here's a pair of proper rascals! One bets he'll take the sheet, and the other writes to stop him winning. If I didn't know for sure that Harry and Freddy were in prison I'd think it was them!'

That night the two rogues crept up through the hemp field. Harry leant a ladder against the window so that Jack would hear him, and climbed up, holding in front of him a straw dummy that looked like a man. When Jack inside heard the ladder being put into place he slipped quietly out of bed and stood beside the window with a big stick. 'This is the best kind of pistol,' he said to his wife, 'it's always loaded.' And when he saw the dummy's head come wobbling up towards him he thought, 'Here he comes,' flung open the window and gave it an almighty crack over the head so that Harry dropped the dummy and gave a loud scream. Meanwhile Freddy was standing as quiet as a mouse by the front door. Carrot-Top Jack heard the scream and then suddenly it was all quiet, and he said, 'Wife, I think something may be wrong, I'd better go down and see!' As he went out of the front door Freddy slipped from behind it into the house and up to the bed, and once again as in the earlier story when they stole the pig (and it is just as true this time) he imitated Jack's voice. 'Wife,' he said, sounding anxious, 'that fellow is as dead as mutton, and just imagine, it's the mayor's son! Quick, give me the sheet and I'll carry him away in it into the forest and bury him there, otherwise we're for the high jump!' She took fright, sat up and gave him the sheet. Hardly had he gone when the real Jack came back and said, very much relieved, 'It was only a silly trick! The thief was a straw dummy.' But when his wife asked, 'What have you done with the sheet then?' and he saw that she was lying on the bare straw mattress, Jack's eyes were at last opened and he said, 'Oh, you damned rascals! It must be Freddy and Harry after all, it can't be anybody else!'

But on the way home Freddy said to Harry, 'Let's call it all off from now on, brother. Everything you get in jail is bad, unless you count good beatings, and from the narrow window there you can see that you-know-what by the road and it doesn't look as though it's any fun to dangle from it!' So Freddy too became an honest man again. But Harry said, 'I'm not packing it in just yet.'

The Clever Sultan

As he was about to go to church one Friday the Grand Sultan of the Turks was approached by one of his subjects, a poor man with a dirty beard, a tattered coat and holes in his slippers. He folded his arms in respectful greeting and said, 'Almighty Sultan, do you believe what the Holy Prophet says?' The Sultan, who was a kindly man, said, 'Yes, I believe what the Prophet says!' The poor man continued, 'The Prophet says in the Koran, "All Muslims are brothers". So, brother, please be so good and share your inheritance with me!' The Sultan smiled and thought, 'This is a new way of asking for alms!' and gave him a silver thaler. The Turk looked long and hard at the coin, first one side then the other. Then he shook his head and said, 'Brother, why do I get one shabby thaler when you have more gold and silver than can be loaded on a hundred mules, and my children at home are so hungry they gnaw at their nails and I shall soon have forgotten that jaws are meant for chewing with? Do you call that sharing with your brother?' But the kindly Sultan wagged a warning finger and said, 'Be satisfied, brother, and don't tell anyone how much I gave you, for ours is a large family, and if all our other brothers come to ask me for their share of the inheritance there won't be enough to go round and you will have to give something too!' His brother took the point and went to Abu Tlengi the baker and bought a loaf of bread for his children while the Sultan went into church and said his prayers.

A Shave as an Act of Charity

A poor man with a black beard came into a barber's shop and asked, for the love of God, not for a piece of bread, but a shave: would the barber kindly take off his beard so that he looked like a decent Christian again? The barber picked up his worst razor, thinking, 'Why should I blunt a good one when he's paying less than nothing?' While he was scraping and hacking away at the poor wretch, who couldn't complain since the bad job was being done for nothing, the dog started howling in the yard outside. 'What's up with Rover,' said the barber, 'to make him whine and howl like that?' 'I don't know,' said Mike. 'Don't ask me,' said Johnny. But the poor devil under the razor said, 'He must be being shaved for the love of God too, like me.'

A Secret Beheading

Whether or not on that morning of 17 June that year the executioner at Landau said the Lord's Prayer with proper devotion and its 'Lead us not into temptation but deliver us from evil' – that I don't know. But a delivery came, a note posted from Nancy, and if he hadn't said his prayers, then it arrived on just the right day. The note said: 'Executioner at Landau, come to Nancy straight away and bring your big sword. You will be told what to do and paid well.' A coach was waiting outside. 'It's my job', thought the executioner and got into the coach. When he was still one hour this side of Nancy, it was evening already and the sun was setting among blood-red clouds, the driver drew up, saying, 'It will be fine again tomorrow', when suddenly three strong armed men were standing by the road, climbed in beside the executioner and promised that he wouldn't come to any harm, 'But you must let us blindfold you!' And when they had put the blindfold over his eyes they said, 'Driver, drive on!' The coachman drove on, and it seemed to the executioner that he was taken a good twelve hours further, and he had no way of telling where he was. He heard the midnight owls; he heard the cocks crow; he heard the morning bells. Then without warning the coach stopped again. They took him into a house and gave him something to drink and a nice roll and sausage too. When he was strengthened by food and drink they led him on inside the same building, through several doors and up stairs and down, and then they removed his blindfold and he saw he was in a large room. It was hung all around with black drapes, and wax candles burnt on the tables. In the middle sat a woman on a chair with her neck bared and a mask over her face, and she must have been gagged, for she couldn't speak, only sob. Round the walls stood a number of gentlemen dressed in black and with black crape over their faces so that the executioner could not have recognized them if he had met them again an hour later. And one of them handed him his sword and ordered him to cut off the head of the woman sitting on the chair. The poor executioner's blood ran cold and he said they must excuse him: his sword was dedicated to the service of justice and he could not defile it with murder. But one of the gentlemen by the wall pointed a pistol at him and said, 'Get on with it! Do as we tell you or you'll never set eyes on the church tower at Landau again!' The executioner thought of his wife and children at home. 'If I've no choice,' he said, 'and I must shed innocent blood, then on your head be it!' and with one blow he severed the poor woman's head from her body.

When it was done one of the men gave him a purse with two

hundred doubloons. They put the blindfold over his eyes again and took him back to the coach he had come in. The men who had brought him there escorted him again. And when at last the coach drew up and they let him get out and remove the blindfold he was left standing where the three men had joined the coach, one hour this side of Nancy on the Landau road, and it was night. The coach sped off back.

That is what happened to the executioner at Landau, and Your Family Friend is not sorry that he can't say who that poor soul was who had to take such a bloody way to life everlasting. No, nobody found out who she was, what sin she had committed, and nobody knows where she is buried.

The Starling from Segringen

A starling may find it useful to have learnt something, but a man even more so.

The barber in a very reputable village – I shall call it Segringen, though it didn't happen there, but hereabouts, and the one it happened to (the man, not the starling) is perhaps reading this right now – the barber at Segringen had a starling, and his apprentice, who's well-known in the district, taught him to speak. The starling not only learnt all the words set in these language lessons but also of his own accord copied what he heard his master say, for example, 'I'm the barber in Segringen.' His owner had other expressions as well that he repeated on every occasion, for example, 'So so, la la', or 'par compagnie' (that means in company with others); or 'God's will be done!' or 'You fool!' You see, that's what he used to call the apprentice when he poured half the plaster on to the table instead of the cloth, or sharpened the back of the razor instead of the edge, or broke a medicine glass. In time the starling learnt all these phrases. The barber also sold brandy, so there were many customers in his shop every day, and often there was much to laugh about when they were talking among themselves and the starling threw in a phrase and it fitted just as if he knew what it meant. And sometimes when the apprentice called to him, 'What are you doing, Johnny?' he answered, 'You fool!', and everyone in those parts could tell you about Johnny! Then one day when his clipped feathers had grown again and the window was open and the weather fine the starling thought: 'I know enough by now to get by in the big world outside', and he was out of the window in a flash. His first flight took him to the fields where he joined a flock of other birds, and when they flew up he went with them, for he thought, 'They know the lie of the land better than I do.' But unfortunately they all flew together into a net. The starling said, 'God's will be done!' When the birdcatcher came and saw what a big catch he had made he took the birds out carefully one by one, wrung their necks and threw them on the ground. But when all unsuspectingly he stretched his murdering hands towards one more catch, that catch cried, 'I'm the barber in Segringen.' Just as if he knew it would save his neck! The birdcatcher was scared at first, thinking something really weird was happening, but then when he had recovered from his shock he laughed so much he nearly died. And when he said, 'Johnny, I didn't expect to find you here, how did you get into my net?' Johnny replied, 'Par compagnie.' So the birdcatcher took the starling back to its owner and was well rewarded for his find. The barber's business prospered, for everybody wanted to see the remarkable Johnny, and now everyone from miles around who wants to be bled goes to the barber at Segringen.

Remember: Such things seldom happen to starlings. But many a young fellow who felt like spreading his wings and getting away from home has got into a mess 'par compagnie' and not got out of it.

You get as much as you give

A man came into an inn with an air of great importance, but few signs of civility. Those inside all doffed their hats or caps to him, except for one who didn't notice him enter because he was busy counting the tricks he had won from his neighbour at a game of 'mariage'. And he was just fingering the ace of hearts, saying,

'Fifty-two and eleven makes sixty-three,' still not noticing the newcomer, evidently a man of some importance, when this stranger asked him, 'You sir, what do you take me for?' The card-player said, 'You're a decent fellow, I suppose; but who may you be?' The stranger said, 'The devil take your cheek!' Then the card-player stood up from the table and asked, 'And what do you, sir, take me for?' The stranger said, 'A lout!' At that the card-player said, 'The devil take you too! I see that we have both misjudged our man!' But now when the others saw that a well-cut coat can cover an ill-bred man they all put their hats on again, and there was nothing the stranger could do about it except be more civil in future.

Well Replied

You must be prepared to take as good as you give!

Once a man was riding past an inn, and he had a splendid paunch on him that almost covered his saddle on both sides. The innkeeper was standing on the steps and called after him: 'Hey, my good fellow, why have you tied your pack in front of you instead of behind?' The horseman shouted back, 'So that I can keep an eye on it. There are scoundrels behind!' The innkeeper had no answer to that.

The Mistaken Reckoning

Rich and important people sometimes have the good fortune to hear, from their servants at least, the truth that others would hardly tell them.

A man who thought highly of himself and his worth, and particularly of the fine outfit he had just put on to go to a wedding, was admiring himself and his fat red cheeks in the mirror when he turned away from the glass to his valet who was watching him approvingly from one side. 'Well, Bob,' he asked, 'what do you think I'm worth as I stand here before you now?' Bob pulled a face as if he had to reckon the value of half a kingdom; for a while he waved his right hand, fingers outstretched, this way and that. 'It must be a good five hundred and fifty guilders,' he said, 'given that everything is dearer these days.' Then his master said, 'You stupid fellow, can't you see that this outfit I'm wearing is worth five hundred guilders alone?' At this the valet retreated a few paces towards the door and said, 'Forgive me if I got it wrong, I reckoned it worth a bit more, otherwise I would not have reached so high a figure.'

The Last Word

A man and his wife lived together in a village on the Danube this side of Ulm, but they weren't cut out for each other, their marriage wasn't made in heaven. She spent money like water and had a wicked tongue; he was mean with everything that didn't go straight down his throat and into his stomach. When he called her a spendthrift she cursed him for a skinflint, and it was up to him how often each day he was honoured with that title. For if he said 'Spendthrift!' a hundred times an hour, she said 'You skinflint!' a hundred and one times, and she always had the last word. Once when they were going to bed they started at it again, and it is said they carried on until five o'clock in the morning, and when in the end they were so tired that they couldn't keep their eyes open and her tongue was longing to nod off, she scratched at her arm with short brisk strokes of her thumb and said yet again, 'You skinflint!' This made him lose all interest in work and in the home and he escaped as soon as he could and went – need you ask where? – to the inn. And what do you think he did there? First he had a drink or two, then he played cards, and finally he got drunk, for cash to begin with, then on credit. For when the woman doesn't make ends meet and the man brings nothing in, their purse may just as well have a hole in it, for there's nothing to fall out of it. But when he had drunk his fill in the Red Horse for the last time and couldn't pay the bill and the landlord chalked up his debt, seven guilders fifty-one kreuzers, on the bar door, he went home, and as soon as he laid eyes on his wife he said to her, 'Insults and disgrace, that's all I get from you, you spendthrift!' 'And all I get from you is trouble and shame, you drunkard, you so and so, you skinflint!' said she. Then black wrath seethed in his heart and those twin devils within him, anger and drink, said to him, 'Throw the bitch into the Danube!' He didn't have to be told twice. 'You wait, I'll show you, you spendthrift!' ('You skinflint!' she answered) 'I'll show you where you belong!', and he carried her down into the Danube. And when her mouth was under but her ears still above water the brute yelled yet again, 'You spendthrift!' At this the woman raised her arms out of the water and with her right thumb she scratched at her left wrist, rubbing briskly as you do when striking a flint, and that was the last thing she did.

You, good reader, set store by what is right and just and you'll not be told that the cruel murderer is still alive! No, he went home and hanged himself by a beam that same night.

Well Spoken, Badly Behaved

A farmer on a nobleman's estate met the village schoolmaster in the fields. 'Schoolmaster, do you still stand by what you were telling the children yesterday: "Whosoever shall smite thee on thy right cheek, turn to him the other also"?' The schoolmaster said, 'I can't change a word of it! It's written in the gospel!' So the farmer boxed his ears, both of them, for he had a longstanding grudge against him. Meanwhile the nobleman was riding by a little way off with his gamekeeper. 'Go and see what those two are up to over there, Joseph!' And as Joseph came up, the schoolmaster, who was a sturdy fellow, boxed the farmer's ears twice too, saying, 'It is also written: "With the same measure that ye mete withal it shall be measured to you again. Good measure, pressed down, and shaken together, and running over, shall men give into your bosom"!' And with that text he gave him another half dozen good blows to the side of his head. Joseph went back to his master and said, 'There's nothing to worry about, sir, they're only discussing Holy Scripture among themselves!'

Remember: You must not try to argue about Holy Scripture if you don't understand it, least of all the way they did. For that same night the nobleman had the farmer locked up for a week; and the schoolmaster, who should have had more sense and more respect for the Bible, was sent packing when school closed in the spring.

The Patient Husband

A man came home tired one evening and was looking forward to a piece of bread and butter with chives on it or a bit of smoked shoulder. But his wife, who wore the trousers in their house and most especially in the kitchen, had the key to the larder in her pocket and was out visiting a friend. So he sent first the maid and then the lad to ask his wife to come home or send him the key. Each time she said, 'I'm just coming, tell him to wait just a moment!' But then, as his hunger grew and his patience dwindled within him, he and the lad carried the locked larder cupboard over to the friend's house where his wife was and he said to her, 'Wife, kindly unlock the cupboard so that I can have something for supper, I can't hold out any longer!' So his wife laughed and cut him off a hunk of bread and a piece of shoulder.

The Cunning Husband

Another man had taken to staying on at the pub until after midnight, so at ten o'clock one night his wife locked the door and went to bed and he was forced, like it or not, to spend the night under the beehive in the garden. The next day – what do you suppose he did? When he went off to the pub he lifted the front door off its hinges and took it with him, and at one o'clock in the morning when he came home he hung it back in place and locked it, and after that his wife never again shut him out and went to bed, but used love and sweetness to mend his ways.

Harry and the Miller from Brassenheim

One day Harry was sitting in an inn, all downcast and thinking of how first Carrot-Top Jack and then his own brother had left him and how he was all on his own now. No, he thought, there's scarcely anyone you can trust any more, and just when you think someone is really straight it turns out he's a scoundrel! Meanwhile several other customers came in and sat down to drink the new wine. 'Have you heard,' said one, 'that Harry Tinder is at large, and tomorrow they'll be out beating the countryside for him, and the magistrate and the clerks are waiting for him to come their way?' When he heard that our Harry felt queer inside, for he thought someone had recognized him and he was done for. But another said, 'It's another of those false rumours again! Doesn't everybody know that Harry and his brother are in the jail at Wollenstein?' Just then the miller from Brassenheim, with his chubby red cheeks and little smiling eyes, rode up on a well-fed grey. And when he came in, and had drunk to the health of the group sitting over their new wine and found that they were talking about Harry Tinder, he said: 'I've heard so many stories about this fellow Harry Tinder! I'd like to clap eyes on him myself one day.' One of them said: 'Watch out that he doesn't come your way all too soon! They say he's on the loose again.' But the miller with his chubby cheeks said: 'Bah! I'll be out of the Fridstadt forest long before nightfall and then I'll be on the main road, and if it comes to the push I'll dig my spurs into my grey.' When Harry heard that he asked the innkeeper's wife, 'What do I owe you?' and off he went to the Fridstadt forest. On the way he met a soldier with a wounded leg on the cart for beggars. 'Let me have your crutch for sixpence,' he said to the

soldier. 'I've twisted my left ankle, and if I put any weight on it it makes me cry out in pain. The coach builder in the next village where you'll be put down will make you a new one.' And so the beggar gave him his crutch. Soon after that two drunken soldiers passed him, singing 'The Cavalrymen's Song'. When he came to the Fridstadt forest he hung the crutch high up on a branch, sat down by the road about six paces away, and tucked in his left leg under him as if he were lame. Now the miller came trotting up on his fine grey, and his expression seemed to say, 'Aren't I the rich miller, the handsome miller, the clever miller?' But when the clever miller rode up to our Harry, Harry said in a voice full of misery: 'Have pity on a poor fellow who can't walk! Two drunken soldiers, you must have seen them, took all the alms I had, and they were angry it was so little and threw my crutch up into that tree there, and it stuck in the branches so that I was left stranded here. Would you be so kind and knock it down with your whip?' The miller said, 'Yes, I met them at the top of the wood. They were singing "My darling Lisa, she's the sweetest girl in all the world".' The miller had to get off his horse and cross over a ditch by a plank to get to the tree and bring down the crutch. He was standing beneath the tree looking up into it when Harry swooped like an eagle on to the fine grey, dug his heels into its sides and rode away. 'Have a nice walk,' he called back to the miller, 'and when you get home tell your wife Harry Tinder sends his greetings!' But when a quarter of an hour after dusk he rode into Brassenheim and came to the mill, and all its wheels were clanking round so that nobody heard him, he jumped off, left the miller's grey tied up at his front door, and went on on foot.

The Fake Gem

Outside the Butcher's Gate at Strassburg there is a pleasant garden where anyone can go and spend his money on decent pleasure, and there sat a well-dressed man drinking his wine like everyone else, and he had a ring with a precious stone on his finger and held it so it sparkled. So a Jew came up and said, 'Sir, you have a lovely gem in that ring on your finger, I wouldn't mind that myself! Doesn't it glitter like the Urim and Thummim in the breastplate of Aaron the priest?' The well-dressed stranger answered very curtly, 'The gem is a fake. If it weren't, it would be on someone else's finger, not mine!' The Jew asked to take a closer look at it. He turned it this way and that in his hand and bent his head to look at it from every angle. 'He says this stone is a fake?' he thought, and offered the stranger two new doubloons for the ring. But the stranger said quite angrily, 'Why do you think I'm lying? I told you, it's a fake!' The Jew asked permission to show it to an expert, and someone sitting close by said, 'I'll vouch for the Israelite, he'll know what the jewel is worth!' The stranger said, 'I don't need to consult anyone, the stone's a fake.'

While this was happening Your Family Friend was sitting at another table in the same garden with good friends of his, happily spending money on decent pleasure, and one of the company was a goldsmith who knows all about gems. He fitted a soldier who lost his nose at the battle of Austerlitz with a silver one and painted it skin colour, and it was a good nose. The only thing he couldn't do was breathe the breath of life into it. The Jew came over to this goldsmith. 'Sir,' he said, 'would you say this is a fake stone? Can King Solomon have worn anything more splendid in his crown?' The goldsmith, who was also something of a star-gazer, said, 'It shines like Aldebaran in the sky all right. I'll get you ninety doubloons for this ring. If you come by it cheaper the profit is yours.'

The Jew went back to the stranger. 'Fake or not, I'll give you six doubloons!' and he counted them out on the table, sparkling new from the mint. The stranger put the ring back on his finger and said, 'I have no intention of parting with it. If it's such a good fake that you think it's real that doesn't make it worth any less to me,' and he put his hand in his pocket so that the eager Israelite could no longer see the stone. 'Eight doubloons.' 'No.' 'Ten doubloons.' 'No.' 'Twelve – fourteen – fifteen doubloons.' 'Very well,' said the stranger at last, 'if you won't leave me in peace and insist on being deceived at all costs! But I tell you, in front of all these gentlemen here, the stone is a fake, and I'll not say it isn't. For I don't want any trouble. You can have the ring, it's yours.'

Now the Jew took the ring joyfully over to the goldsmith. 'I'll come for the money tomorrow.' But the goldsmith, who had never been taken in by anyone, opened his eyes wide in amazement. 'My friend, this isn't the ring you showed me two minutes ago! This stone is worth twenty kreuzers at most. This is the sort they make in the glass works at Sankt Blasien!' For actually the stranger had in his pocket a fake ring which looked as good as the one that had first sparkled on his finger, and while the Jew was bargaining with him and his hand was in his pocket, he pushed the genuine ring off his finger with his thumb and slipped his finger into the fake, and that was the one he had given the Jew. At once the dupe shot back to the stranger as if fired on a rocket: 'Oh, woe, woe unto me! I have been tricked, the stone is a fake!' But the stranger said coldly and calmly, 'I sold it to you for a fake. These gentlemen here are witnesses. It's yours now. Did I talk you into buying it or did you talk me into selling it?' All those present had to admit, 'Yes, he told you the stone was a fake when he said you could have it!' So the Jew had to keep the ring and no further fuss was made of the matter.

The Cunning Girl

A number of rich and distinguished gentlemen were enjoying a day out in a large town. One of them thought, 'If we can spend fifteen hundred guilders or more at the inn and on the musicians then we can give something for the poor too.' So it was that when they were at their merriest a pretty, neatly dressed girl came up with a plate and with winning smiles and charming words asked for alms for the poor. All of them gave, some more, some less, according to the size of his purse and his heart. For small purse and tight heart give little, large purse and big heart give in plenty. The man the girl now approached had a big heart. For when he looked into her sparkling, appealing eyes he almost lost it to her. So he put two louis d'or in the plate and whispered into the girl's ear, 'For your pair of lovely blue eyes!' What he meant was this: Because you, my pretty alms-collector, have such beautiful eyes, I'm giving the poor two beautiful louis d'or, otherwise one would do! But the cunning girl pretended to take his meaning quite differently. For he said, 'For your pair of lovely blue eyes' – and so she very coyly took the two louis d'or from the plate, pocketed them for herself and said with a winning curtsy, 'Thank you kindly, sir! But be so kind and give something for the poor too!' The gentleman then put another two louis d'or in the plate, gave the girl a friendly pinch on the cheek and said, 'You little rascal, you!' But the others made cruel fun of him, and they drank to the girl's health, and the band sounded a flourish.

A Good Prescription

The Emperor Joseph* in Vienna was, as everyone knows, a wise and benevolent monarch, but not everyone knows that he once was a doctor and cured a poor woman.

A poor woman who was ill said to her small son, 'Fetch a doctor, I can't stand the pain any longer!' The little lad ran off to the nearest doctor and then to the next, but they wouldn't come, for in Vienna a visit costs a guilder and the poor lad had nothing but tears, coins that may indeed be accepted in heaven, but not by everybody on earth. But when he was on his way to the third doctor or coming back home again the Emperor was driving slowly by in an open carriage. The boy obviously took him to be a rich man though he didn't know it was the Emperor, and he thought, I'll try him! 'Kind sir,' he said, 'please give me a guilder, do be so kind!' The Emperor thought: he doesn't waste words and thinks if he gets a guilder in one go he won't need to beg for a kreuzer sixty times over! 'Won't a six-kreuzer bit do, or two twenties?' asked the Emperor. The boy said it wouldn't and explained why he needed the money. So the Emperor gave him the guilder and found out from him his mother's name and exactly where she lived, and while the boy was running to fetch the third doctor and the sick woman was praying at home that God should not forsake her, the Emperor drove to her lodgings and drew his cloak around him so that he couldn't be recognized unless you took a close look. But when he came into the sick woman's room, and thoroughly bare and joyless it looked, she thought it was the doctor and told him about her illness and how she was so poor too and couldn't provide for herself. The Emperor said, 'I'll write you out a prescription straight away,' and she told him where to find the boy's pen and paper. So he wrote out the prescription, told her which chemist's to take it to when the boy got back, and left it on the table. Yet he had hardly been gone a minute when the real doctor arrived as well. The woman was not a little surprised when she heard that he was the doctor, and said she was sorry, one had already called and left a prescription, and she was only waiting for her son. The doctor picked up the prescription to see who it was who had called and what sort of potion or pills he had prescribed, and then he too was not a little surprised. 'Well,' he said, 'you're in the hands of a good doctor, for he has prescribed twenty-five doubloons to be collected from the paymaster's and it's signed Joseph, you may have heard of him? I couldn't have prescribed anything half as effective to sort out your stomach and do your heart good and bring a sparkle back into your eyes!' At that the woman cast her eyes towards heaven and was overcome by emotion and speechless with gratitude, and afterwards the money was paid out at the paymaster's all correct and without fuss, and the doctor prescribed a mixture for her, and with the good medicine and the good food she could now afford she was well and on her feet again within a few days. So it was that the doctor cured the sick woman and the Emperor cured the poor woman, and she is still alive and has married again.

Terrible Disasters in Switzerland

Every stretch of land is a good place to live, yet each has its bad side too, and when we sometimes hear of what happens else-where we surely have cause to be happy with our own homeland. Switzerland, for instance, has many mountain pastures rich in cattle, it has cheese and butter and freedom, but it has avalanches too. The 12th of December 1809 brought a terrible night for the high mountain valleys of that land. It teaches us how we all have daily cause to remember the words: 'In the midst of life we are in death.' All the high mountains were covered by a deep fall of fresh snow. That 12th of December brought a thaw and a strong wind. Everyone then feared a great disaster and said their prayers. Those who thought they and their homes were safe were troubled by sadness and fear for the unfortunate people who would suffer, and those who did not feel safe said to their children, 'We shall not see another day,' and prepared to meet their Maker. Then suddenly everywhere great masses of snow broke loose from the highest mountain ridges and came thundering down in avalanches over the long slopes, growing bigger and bigger, gaining in speed, rushing on with an ever more fearful roar, driving the air before them and causing it to gust this way and that, so that even before an avalanche arrived whole forests were felled by the blast, and byres and barns and woodlands were blown away like chaff; and where the avalanches plunged down on to the valley floor whole areas lay crushed under their weight for hours on end, and all the houses and all living creatures that drew breath there were destroyed, but for those who were saved as if by divine miracle.

One of two brothers in Uri who shared the same house was up on the roof facing the mountain behind, planning to pack the space between the roof and the mountainside with snow. 'I'll level it out so that when the avalanche comes it will pass over the house and perhaps we . . .' And as he was about to say, 'perhaps we will escape with our lives', the sudden gust that preceded the avalanche tossed him off the roof and he was carried away through the air, soaring like a bird over a ghastly precipice. And just as he was in danger of crashing down into the bottomless depths where his remains would never have been found, the avalanche swept past him and threw him sideways on to a slope. He says it wasn't a good feeling, yet though stunned he was able to grab a tree and hold fast to it until it was all over, and he escaped unharmed and went back home to his brother, who was also still alive, though the cowshed next to the house had been swept clean away as if by a broom. For this too there are apt words: 'The Lord gave His angels charge over thee to bear thee up in their hands. For He maketh the winds that blow announce His majesty and the avalanches to act according to His will.'

It was a different story in Sturnen, which is in Canton Uri too. After prayers that evening a man said to his wife and their three children, 'We shall ask a special blessing for the poor people who are in danger tonight.' And while they were still knelt in prayer all the valleys echoed with the thunder of distant avalanches, and still they were praying when all at once the barn and the house collapsed. The father was carried off by the rushing wind, out into the terrible darkness and down to the foot of the mountain, and was buried in the snowdrifts. He was still alive, but the next morning when with enormous effort he dug himself free and made his way back to where the house had stood and looked to see what had become of his family, merciful heavens! there was nothing there but snow upon snow, no trace to be found of a house, nor any sign of life. Yet after calling anxiously for some time, from under the snow as if from deep in a grave he heard his wife's voice. And when he had dug her out safe and unharmed, now they heard another dear familiar voice. 'Mother, I think I'm still alive,' a child was calling, 'but I can't get out of here!' So father and mother set to work again and dug out their son too, and he had lost one of his arms. Now their hearts were filled with joy and pain and their eyes shed tears of thanks and sorrow. They found the other two children too, but they were dead.

In Pilzeig, also in Canton Uri, a mother with her two children was swept away and buried deep under the snow. The avalanche had thrown their neighbour down there too, he heard their moans and dug them out. But in vain did their faces shine with hope. When the scantily dressed woman looked around her she no longer recognized her surroundings. Her rescuer had himself fallen in a faint. New hills and mountains of snow and a terrible whirlwind of snowflakes filled the air. Seeing this she said, 'Children, we are lost; let us pray and submit to God's will!' They

were at prayer when the seven-year-old daughter sank dying into her mother's arms. The heartbroken mother, her strength draining from her too, was talking to her, recommending her to God's mercy. She was two weeks into confinement, and she too died, with the dear dead body of her child in her womb. The other daughter, an eleven-year-old, stayed with her mother and sister, weeping and wringing her hands, until they were both dead, then in silent grief she closed their eyes. Only then did she turn her mind to her own escape, with untold effort and through unimaginable danger she hauled herself up to a tree and then to a rock, and at last towards midnight she reached a house and was dragged in through a window, and was safe together with those who lived there.

You have read enough to understand that in all the mountain cantons of Switzerland, in Berne, Glarus, Uri, Schwyz, Graubünden, in that one night, and almost within the space of the same hour, whole families were smothered by avalanches, whole herds and their byres were crushed, pastures, gardens and orchards were swept away, scooped out down to the bare rock, and whole forests were destroyed, flung down into the valley below or the trees tangled, crushed, bent and broken like blades of corn in the fields after a hailstorm. In the one small canton of Uri alone, almost in one fell swoop eleven people were engulfed under the snow never to arise again, thirty or so houses and more than one hundred and fifty hay-sheds were destroyed, three hundred and fifty-nine head of cattle perished, and there was no way of reckoning the damage done in how many hundreds of thousands of guilders, not counting the lives lost. For the life of a father or mother, a godfearing husband or child is not to be measured in gold.

How a Ghastly Story was Brought to Light by a Common or Garden Butcher's Dog

Two butchers out in their district buying in animals came to a village and split up, one went left past the Swan, the other right, and they said, 'We'll meet up again in the Swan.' But they never did meet up again. For one of them went with a farmer into his cowshed. The farmer's wife went as well, though she was doing the washing in the kitchen, and their child decided to follow too. The devil gave the woman a nudge: 'Look at that belt full of money peeping out from under the butcher's shirt!' The woman gave her husband a wink, he gave her a nod, and they killed the poor butcher in the cowshed and hurriedly hid his body under some straw. The devil nudged the woman again: 'Look who's watching!' She looked round and saw the child. So, driven out of their minds by fear, they went back together into the house and locked the doors as if the enemy were near. Then the woman, whose heart was not just as black as sin but blacker and hotter than hell, said, 'Child, just look at you again! Come into the kitchen,' she said, 'I'll clean you up.' In the kitchen she pushed her child's head into the hot suds and scalded him to death. Now, she thought, there's no one to tell on us – but she didn't think of the murdered butcher's dog.

The murdered butcher's dog had run along a bit with the other butcher, and then, while the child was being boiled and then popped into the bread oven, the dog doubled back and picked up his master's scent, sniffed at the cowshed door, scratched at the door to the house, and knew that something was wrong. Off he ran at once, back into the village, looking for the other butcher. Soon he was whinging and whining and pulling at this butcher's coat, and the butcher, too, knew something was wrong. So he went with the dog back to the house, in no doubt that something dreadful had happened there. He beckoned over two men who were passing nearby. When the murderers heard the dog whining and the butcher shouting, they had nothing but the gallows before their eyes and the fear of hellfire in their hearts. The man tried to escape through the back window but his wife grabbed him by his coat and said, 'Stay here with me!' The man said, 'Come with me!' She answered, 'I can't, my legs won't move! Can't you see that ghastly figure outside the window, with its flaming eyes and fiery breath?' Meanwhile the door had been

broken open. They soon found the two corpses. The criminals were taken and brought to court. Six weeks later they were put to death, their villainous corpses bound to the wheel, and even now the crows are still saying, 'That's tasty meat, that is!'

A Strange Divorce

A young Swiss from Balsthal went into Spanish service, did well and earned himself a little fortune. But when he was doing all too nicely he thought, 'Shall I or shan't I?' In the end he decided he would, and took a pretty and well-to-do Spanish girl to wife, and so he put an end to his days of happiness. For in Spanish households the wife is the master, a lover plays the husband, and the husband is the maid.

The poor fellow was soon tired of slavery and persecution, and he began as if by chance to speak to her in praise of the happy life in Switzerland and its golden mountains (he meant the snowy peaks in the sunshine beyond the gorge at Klus), and what a pleasure it was to make the pilgrimage to Einsiedeln, how lovely to pray at the grave of the Holy Brother Nicholas of Flues, and what a great fortune he had there at home, but it couldn't be taken out of the country. In the end the Spanish woman's mouth watered at the thought of that wonderful land and the fortune, and she agreed to turn her property into money and to go with him back to his golden homeland. So they travelled together across the great Pyrenees mountains to the stone that marks the boundary between the kingdom of Spain and France, she on a donkey with the money, he on foot alongside. But when they had passed the boundary stone he said, 'Wife, if you don't mind, up till now we have followed Spanish customs, from now on we'll do things the German way! You have ridden from Madrid to the border and I've trotted after you on foot all the way up the mountain, so I shall ride from here to Balsthal in the canton of Solothurn. Now it's your turn to walk!' Yet she refused to listen, and cursed and threatened and wouldn't get off the animal. 'Woman, you haven't understood yet,' he said then, 'and I can't say I blame you!' But he cut off a good-sized branch by the roadside and used it to teach her a long lesson on the Balsthal laws on marriage and husband's rights, and when she had taken it all in he asked her, 'Will you come with me now, you dago witch, and behave yourself, or will you go back where you come from?' Then she sobbed and said, 'Where I come from', and that was what he wanted to hear. So the honest Swiss shared the fortune with her and they separated at this 'Boundary Stone of Woman's Rights', as a well-known book was called, and they both went

back to their own countries. 'You can take your fellow countryman with you,' he said, 'the one you rode here!'

Remember: In the kingdom of Spain women go too far, but in
Balsthal men do too sometimes! A husband should never beat his
wife, or he brings dishonour on himself. For you are one body.

The Cunning Styrian

It was in Styria during the last war* and some way off the main
road, and a rich farmer was thinking: 'How can I keep my thalers
and my dear little ducats safe in these evil times? I'm ever so fond
of the Empress Maria Theresa, God bless her, and the Emperor
Joseph, God bless him, and the Emperor Francis, God give him
long life and health! And just when you think you have these dear
sovereigns ever so safe and out of harm's way the enemy gets a
whiff of them as soon as he sticks his nose into the village and
takes them off prisoner to Lorraine or Champagne! It's enough to
make a poor patriotic Austrian's heart bleed!' 'I've got it!' he said,
'I know what I'll do,' and in the dark moonless night he took his
money out into the kitchen garden. 'The Seven Sisters will not
betray me,' he said. Out in the garden he put the money straight
down between the wallflowers and the sweet peas. Next to it he
dug a hole in the path between the beds, threw all the soil on top
of the coins and trampled on the beautiful flowers and the chard
all around like someone treading down sauerkraut. The next
Monday the Chasseurs were scouting all round the district, and
on the Tuesday a patrol entered the village and went straight to
the mill, and then with white elbows from the mill to our farmer.
And an Alsatian brandished his sword and bawled at him, 'Out
with your money, farmer, or say your last Our Father!' The

farmer said they were welcome in God's name to take whatever they could find. He had nothing left, it had all gone yesterday and the day before that. 'You'll not find anything,' he said, 'you fine fellows!' When they found nothing except for a couple of coppers and a gilded threepenny piece with the image of the Empress Maria Theresa on it and a ring to hang it up by, the Alsatian said, 'Farmer, you've buried your money! Show us here and now where you buried your money or you'll leave for the hereafter without saying your last Our Father!' 'I can't show you it here and now,' said the farmer, 'I'm sorry, but you'll have to come with me out into the kitchen garden. I'll show you where it was hidden there and what happened. Our lords and masters, the enemy, were here before you, yesterday and the day before, and they found it and took the lot.' The Chasseurs saw how things looked in the garden, found everything just as the man said, and not one of them thought the money might be lying under the pile of earth, but each of them gazed into the empty hole and thought: 'If only I'd been here earlier!' 'And if only they hadn't ruined the wallflowers, and the chard as well!' said the farmer, and so he fooled them and all those who came after them, and so it was that he saved the whole family of archdukes, the Emperor Francis, the Emperor Joseph, the Empress Maria Theresa, and Leopold the First, the Most Blessed of All, and kept them safe in their own country.

A Report from Turkey

There is justice in Turkey. A merchant's man was overtaken on his journey by night and fatigue, tied his horse laden with precious goods to a tree not far from a guardhouse, lay down under the shelter of the tree and went to sleep. Early next day he was woken by the morning air and the quails calling. He had slept well, but his horse had gone.

So he rushed off to the governor of the province, Prince Carosman Oglu he was called and he was staying nearby, and complained that he had been robbed. The prince cut the hearing short: 'So close to the guardhouse! Why didn't you ride on another fifty yards, then you would have been safe! It's your own stupid fault!' But then the merchant's man said, 'O just prince, should I have feared to sleep in the open in a land where you rule?' That pleased the Prince Carosman, and it annoyed him too. 'Drink a little glass of Turkish brandy tonight,' he said to the merchant's man, 'and sleep under the same tree again.' The man did just as he was told. The next morning when he was woken by the morning air and the quails calling he had slept well again, for the horse was standing there tethered at his side together with all the precious goods, and in the tree hung a dead man, the thief, who never saw the sun rise again.

They do say there are trees enough in most parts, big ones and little ones.

How One Day Freddy Tinder Escaped from Prison and Came Safely over the Border

One day Freddy Tinder had found his own way out of prison, thinking, 'I'll not wake the jailor this early,' and arrest warrants were already flying down all the roads ahead of him when in the evening, still unchallenged, he reached a little town on the border. When the sentry there ordered him to stop and to state who he was, his name and his business, Freddy asked him boldly, 'Do you speak Polish?' The sentry said, 'I know a bit of foreign lingo all right. But I don't know that I've come across any Polish among it yet.' 'In that case,' said Freddy, 'we'll have difficulties understanding each other.' Was there an officer or sergeant at the gate? The sentry fetched the guard commander, telling him there was a Pole at the barrier with whom he had communication problems. The commander came out, but at once apologized that he didn't know much Polish either. 'There's not much traffic in these parts,' he said, 'and I don't suppose there's anyone in the whole place who could act as interpreter.' 'If I'd known that,' said Freddy, and looked at the watch which he had found on a coat rack on his way there, 'I would have gone on for another hour or two to the next town. The moon rises at nine.' The officer at the gate said, 'In the circumstances it would almost be better if you went straight through without stopping, it isn't a large town,' and was glad to get rid of him. So it was that Freddy went safely in by the gate. He stayed in the town no longer than was needed to teach a lesson or two to a goose that was late going home. 'You geese,' he said, 'never do as you are told! When evening comes you belong inside or with someone to keep a good eye on you!' And so he grabbed it firmly by the neck and as cool as you please thrust it under the coat that he had likewise borrowed from an unknown benefactor on the way. But when he came to the gate at the other end of town, again he didn't trust them to keep the peace. The soldier inside was stirring. Freddy, three steps from the guard post, called out boldly, 'Who goes there!' The soldier, all good nature, replied, 'Friend!' So it was that Freddy came safely out the other side of the town and over the border.

The Cosy Sentry Box

This sentry box had the usual round openings to look out through on both sides, and they were rather big ones, so that the recruit standing inside found it was just a bit too draughty. So when he had been stood down he asked the corporal if it wouldn't be better to nail them up with a couple of boards. The corporal scratched his beard and said, 'No, that's not on, because of the winter! It's greatcoats outside in winter, shirt-sleeve order in summer.' So the next time he was on sentry duty the recruit pushed his arms out through the holes and said he was beginning to like a soldier's life, seeing as they were concerned for a fellow's comfort after all.

The Lightest Death Sentence

People have said it's the guillotine. But it isn't, you know! A man who had done much for his country and was highly thought of by its ruler was sentenced to death for a crime he'd committed in a fit of passion. Petitions or prayers were no use. But since he was otherwise highly regarded by the ruler, he, the prince, let him choose how he would like to die: he was to die in whatever way he chose. So the chief secretary came to him in prison: 'The prince has determined to show you mercy. If you wish to be put to death on the wheel you shall be put on the wheel; if you wish to be hanged he will have you hanged – there are already two up on the gallows but everybody knows there's room for three at a time. If, however, you would rather take rat poison there is some at the chemist's. For whatever kind of death you choose the prince says it shall be yours. But, as you know, die you must!' The criminal replied, 'If I really must die, then death on the wheel can be bent to suit one's taste, and hanging can be turned to suit one's inclination if the wind lends a hand. But you haven't got the point! For my part I have always thought that death from old age is the easiest way, and since the prince leaves the choice to me I'll choose it and no other!' And that was his final decision, he wouldn't be talked out of it. So they had to let him go free and live on until he died of old age. For the prince said, 'I gave my word and I'll not break it.'

This little story comes from our mother-in-law who doesn't like to let anyone die if she can possibly help it.

The Strange Gent

A tailor in town had let his needles get a little rusty and the blades of his scissors stick together for a few years, so now he kept body and soul together as best he could. 'Neighbour,' the wig-maker said to him, 'You like to take things easy, but perhaps you'll carry a new wig in its box to the deacon at Brassenheim? It's very light and he will make the walk worth your while.' 'All right then,' says the tailor, 'Besides, it's fair time in Brassenheim. Lend me the clothes that gentleman roaming around on horseback left in pawn with you, the one who pulled a fast one on you, and I'll cut a good figure at the fair!'

Now our assistant has this good habit, that if he knows there's a fair less than three hours away and he's been well paid by Your Family Friend, then he spends good money at the stalls that sell the latest ditties and fine Jew's harps from Damascus. So our assistant was sat down in the Green Man at Brassenheim trying out the songs – song number one, 'A Little Lamb was Drinking', number two, 'A Fine Young Stag is Bounding', number three, 'There is No Finer Life', and testing the harps. All at once in came the tailor in a red coat, deerskin trousers, half boots with tassels on them, and a pair of spurs. The landlord doffed his cap politely, the customers too, and mine-host asked him, 'Has the lad put your horse in the stable, sir?' 'My thoroughbred Norman, the piebald?' said the tailor. 'I left him au cerf, at the Stag's Head. I've just come to try your wine. I'm the famous Adelstan, on my travels collecting facts about men and wine. Move aside!' he says to our assistant. Aha! thought the assistant, here's another fellow who believes rudeness is a mark of quality. I wouldn't mind betting he isn't far from home! When the tailor flung his switch down across the table and cleared his throat like a camel and viewed the company through a burning glass, and the assistant with it, the assistant got slowly to his feet and said something quietly in the landlord's ear. A man from Ehningen, hearing him, said, 'You're on the right track all right! I saw him washing his boots by the stream and cutting himself a switch. He came here on foot.' A scissors-sharpener said, 'I think I know him, he used to be a tailor. He doesn't work any more and runs errands for others.' Now the landlord went out for a minute and then came back. 'It seems we can't have a fair here without an accident,' he said as he came in again. 'The bailiffs are out looking in all the inns for a gent in a red coat who galloped through the villages earlier today and rode down a child and killed it.' All the customers were looking at Sir Adelstan, and he was scared and blurted out, 'My coat isn't red, it's brown!' But the man from Ehningen said, 'It's red all right, yet your face has changed colour, it's gone white, and there's a sudden shower of sweat on it! Own up, you didn't come on horseback!' 'But he did ride here all right!' said the landlord, 'I've just tethered his mount outside. It broke loose from the Stag's Head and was looking for him. Your fine steed does have his mane under his chin, doesn't he, and cloven hoofs, and when he bleats wouldn't you just take him for a horse? Pay for your wine now, and ride properly on your way back home!' But when the tailor stepped outside and saw the animal that the landlord had tied up by the door he wouldn't get on its back, instead he left the village on Shanks's pony, with those at the inn jeering after him horribly.

Remember: You must never pretend to be more than you are or what you can hope to keep up, for the future will tell.

Field Marshal Suvorov

The piece about Suvorov obeying his own orders went down well with you, good readers. Many good things could be said about him.

If an important person is not arrogant but deigns to speak to ordinary folk and sometimes behaves as if he were one of them, then we approve and call him a man of the people. Suvorov was in a position to pin many shining decorations on his breast, he could choose from many diamond rings to put on his fingers and take a pinch of snuff from several gold snuffboxes. After all, he was victorious in Poland and Turkey wasn't he, a Russian field marshal and prince, at the head of 300,000 men? Few could compare with him! But for all that he was a man of the people.

When he didn't have to he didn't wear a general's uniform but whatever he pleased. Sometimes he had only one boot on when he gave his orders. His stocking was rolled down on the other leg and his breeches flapped loose. He had a gammy knee, you see.

Often he was even less well dressed. In the morning, no matter how cold it was, he rose from his bed or the straw and walked out of his tent in his birthday suit and had a couple of buckets of cold water poured over him to freshen him up.

He had no valet or heyduck, just a manservant, no carriage and no special mount. He took any old horse to ride into battle.

He ate what the common soldiers ate. It was no great joy to be invited to dine with him! He would often visit the common soldiers in their tents and behave like one of them.

If on the march, or in camp or wherever, he was moved to do what others go behind a tree or a hedge to do, he made no fuss. Those who hadn't seen such a thing before were welcome to watch.

On great occasions, when he stood arrayed in his fine marshal's uniform covered in medals and insignia, and whatever bit of him you looked at was all gleaming and jingling with gold and silver, he behaved like a farmer who keeps himself clean and throws away what a fine gentleman puts in his pocket. He blew his nose with his fingers, wiped them on his sleeve, and straight away took another pinch from his gold snuffbox.

That's how he was, the General, Prince Italyski Suvorov.*

A Stallholder is Duped

A rouble is a silver coin in Russia, worth a bit less than two guilders, whereas an imperial is a gold coin and worth ten roubles. So you can get a rouble for an imperial, for instance if you lose nine roubles at cards, but you can't get an imperial for a rouble. Yet a cunning soldier in Moscow said, 'Want to bet? Tomorrow at the fair I'll get me an imperial for a rouble.' The next day long rows of stalls were set out at the fair, the people were already standing at all the booths, admiring or finding fault, making bids and haggling, the crowd was walking up and down and the boys were saying hello to the girls, when up came the soldier with a rouble in his hand. 'Whose is this rouble? Is it yours?' he asked all the stallkeepers in turn. One of them who wasn't doing much business looked on for some time and then thought: if that money's too hot for you to hold I can warm to it! 'Over here, musketeer, it's my rouble!' The soldier said, 'If you hadn't shouted I would never have found you in the crowd,' and he handed him the rouble. The trader turned it one way and the other and tested its ring; it was a good one all right, and he put it in his purse. 'Now give me back my imperial, please!' said the musketeer. The trader said, 'I don't have any imperial of yours, I owe you nothing. You can have this stupid rouble back if you're playing a trick on me!' But the musketeer said, 'Hand over my imperial, this is no joke, I'm serious and can easily fetch a constable!' One thing led to another, a polite word to a defiant one, defiance to insults, and a crowd gathered around the stall like bees round a honey pot. Then something was burrowing its way through the throng. 'What's going on here?' said the police sergeant who had pushed through the crowd with his men. 'I said, what's all this?' The stallkeeper couldn't say much, but the musketeer had a good story to tell.

Less than a quarter of an hour before, he said, he had bought this and that from this man for one rouble. But when it came to paying he could find only a double imperial, nothing smaller, one his godfather had given him when he was enlisted. So he gave him the imperial until he came back with a rouble. When he came back with the rouble he couldn't find the right stall, so he asked at all the booths, 'Who do I owe a rouble?' And this man said it was him, and it was too, and he took the rouble but pretended he didn't have his imperial. 'Now will you agree to give it back?' The police sergeant questioned those around and they said: Yes, the musketeer asked at all the stalls whose rouble it was and this man said it was his, and took it too, and tested it to see if it was genuine. When the police sergeant heard that, he settled the matter: 'You've got your rouble, so give this soldier his imperial or we'll close down your stall and nail it up with you inside and leave you to starve to death!' Thus the police officer, and the trader it was who had to give the musketeer an imperial for a rouble.

Remember: Other people's property can eat into your own just as fresh snow swallows up the old.

An Officer's Wife is Saved

Things sometimes have to get pretty violent and bloody before you can recognize a noble frame of mind where you don't expect it.

In the Tyrol things were pretty violent and bloody during the last war.* They had just murdered a Bavarian staff officer, and their swords and dung forks were wet with blood as they pushed into the room where his wife was, weeping with her child in her lap, telling God of her grief, and they were going to murder her too. 'Oh yes,' screamed one of them in his rage, and he was the worst of the lot, 'you're done for now, and that brat of yours there has Bavarian blood in its veins too! You will die within the hour, first that little devil of yours and then you! Give her an hour,' he said to the others, 'to say her prayers; she is a Christian and a Catholic.'

But a quarter of an hour later she was praying alone when he came back and said, 'Lady, it's me again, but please, don't be afraid and don't be angry at what I said, I meant well by you. Let me take your child under my cloak so I can smuggle him away to my mother's, and you yourself put on these things here,' and with that he took them out from under his cloak, 'and so help me God and Our Lady, I'll see if I can save you too!' When he had taken the child to safety and came back she was ready dressed in the Tyrolean man's clothes. He pulled the broad hat well down over her face, put her braces to rights and placed a dung fork in her hand just as if she were a rebel in mine-host Hofer's lifeguards and halberdiers. 'Now then, in God's name,' he said, 'follow me, and put your feet down firmly as you leave, and push your shoulders back and your elbows out!' As they went down the stairs together the others were coming up again. 'Have you done for her already, Joe?' one asked him. But he said, 'No, she locked the door and was saying her prayers. She may be finished by now. When I peeped through the keyhole she was just getting to her feet.' So as he went down the stairs with her the others pushed up past them, and while they banged and hammered at the locked door and were bawling, 'Have you done? We'll kick the door in if you don't hurry up!' into the empty room, he took her to his mother's and gave her back her child, and the baby boy smiled, and she wept and pressed him fervently against her cheek and to her breast. So happily and with God's help the noble Tyrolean had saved her from the hands of her murderers, and later he led her through the night by secret paths till they found a Bavarian picket just as the sun was rising.

Andreas Hofer

During the last war when the French and the Austrians had their
work cut out dealing with each other in the region of the Tyrol,
the Tyroleans thought, 'There's good fishing to be had in
troubled waters.' They didn't want to be Bavarian any longer.*
Many heads make for many opinions, sometimes none at all.
When it came to it they themselves didn't really know what they
wanted. But now the bells were ringing the alarm in every valley.
From every mountain the marksmen came down with their
carbines. Young and old, men and women reached for their
weapons. The Bavarians and the French had a hard time of it,
especially in the narrow passes when rocks rained down on them
the size of small houses. The rebels' fortunes varied from
encounter to encounter. They took Innsbruck, the capital of the
Tyrol, then had to abandon it; they won it back again, and yet
couldn't keep it. Monstrous cruel things were done, and not only
to the Bavarian officials and citizens, but to their fellow
countrymen too. Like it or lump it! Anyone who refused to go
along with them put his life at risk – Harry the gamekeeper could
tell you all about that if he were still alive! In the end, when many
a fine village and town lay in ashes, many a man of means was
made a beggar, many a thoughtless and crazed fellow had lost his
life, and when every village, almost every home, had its corpses,
its wounds and its misery, then finally they said to themselves that
being Bavarian was after all better than they had at first thought,
and they submitted once more. You can't tell until you've tried it!
Only a few madcaps preferred to be shot or hanged a bit first –
Andreas Hofer, for instance.

Andreas Hofer kept the Sand Inn at Passeier and dealt in

cattle, and up to his fortieth year when the uprising broke out he poured out many a glass of wine, used up many a piece of chalk listing bad debts, and he could judge a head of cattle as well as anyone. But in the revolt he rose to be commander, not just of a town or valley but of the whole principality of the Tyrol; and he set up his quarters, not just in a parsonage or a magistrate's house but in the great palace, the residence of princes in Innsbruck. Before long he had some 50,000 reservists under his command. Those who had no guns presented arms with a pitchfork. Anything that was decreed and drawn up over the name of Andreas Hofer had the force of law. His privy minister of war was a gentleman of the church, Father Joachim by name; his adjutant, mine host from the Crown at Bludenz; his secretary, a runaway student. Under his rule 30,000 guilders' worth of Tyrolean thirty-kreuzer coins were minted, Your Family Friend is one of those who has a hatful of them. He even set up his own cannon foundry – and how do you suppose that was done? The cannon were bored from logs and bound around with strong iron hoops. And yes, their effect was great and not just on the enemy! In Innsbruck he did himself proud. You get fat on your own cooking, and he said, 'I've played host long enough. Now I'll let others wait on me for a change!' For all that he never changed his manner of dress. He went around clothed like any ordinary Tyrolean and his beard was as long as it would grow. He just wore a pair of pistols in his red belt and a long heron's feather in his green hat, and alongside his onerous duties as ruler he went on dealing in cattle as before. One minute he sent his adjutant with orders to the army, the next in came the butcher: 'What are you asking for the four bullocks you have up at your brother-in-law's?' He wasn't simply a brute. He prevented much suffering, where he could. He told an officer

who had been taken prisoner, 'You'll be shot tomorrow!' The next day he said, 'I'm told you are a good fellow, I'll give you a pass so that you can go back home.' But greater was the suffering he brought about by his stubbornness in refusing all offers of peace, and by his perfidy. At one time he wrote to the Bavarian High Command, 'We surrender and beg for mercy. Andere Hofer, Supream Comarnder in Tiroll as was.' At the same time he wrote to his adjutant, mine host of the Crown, 'Hold out as long as you can. While there's life there's hope!' But when in the end the misguided people gave in and accepted the mercy offered them by their magnanimous king, and all those who after that were then found carrying the weapons of rebellion were hanged and many a tree bore such a fruit, Andreas Hofer was not to be found at home nor on a tree; and it was said that he had taken a little walk over the border. He may well have been planning to do that, in his wretched wooden herdsman's hut high on a mountain in the furthest Passeier valley where he and his secretary were in hiding surrounded by six-foot walls of snow. His house and belongings had been plundered by the furious peasants. Now and then meagre rations were got to him by his wife who, with her five children, now lived on the charity of others. Now things were not as they had been in the palace at Innsbruck. But worse awaited him. One of his good friends betrayed his whereabouts for money. A French detachment surrounded his hut and took him prisoner. He was found with four loaded muskets, a deal of money, but little food. He was thin from want, worry and fear. And so he was taken by a strong military escort, to the beat of a drum, across the country into Italy and to the prison at Mantua, and there he was shot. That's what you get from fishing in troubled waters.

Those who don't look before they leap often find it's grief they reap.

Patience Rewarded

One day a Frenchman rode up on to a bridge over a stream, and it was so narrow there was scarcely room for two horses at once. An Englishman was riding up from the other side, and when they met in the middle neither of them would give way. 'An Englishman does not make way for a Frenchman!' said the Englishman. 'Pardieu,' said the Frenchman, 'My horse has an English pedigree too! It's a pity I can't turn him round and let you have a good look at his backside in retreat! But you could at least let that English fellow you're riding step aside for this English mount of

mine. In any case yours seems to be the junior; mine served under Louis XIV in the battle of Kieferholz, 1702!'*

But the Englishman was not greatly impressed. 'I have all the time in the world!' he said. 'This gives me a chance to read today's paper until you are pleased to make way.' So with the coolness the English are famed for he took a newspaper from his pocket and opened it up and sat on his horse on the bridge and read for an hour, and the sun didn't look as if it would shine on this pair of fools for ever, it was going down quickly towards the mountains. An hour later when he had finished reading and was about to fold up the newspaper again he looked at the Frenchman and said, 'Eh bien?' But the Frenchman had kept his head too and replied, 'Englishman, kindly lend me your paper a while, so that I can read it too until you are pleased to make way.' Now, when the Englishman saw that his adversary was a patient man, he said,

'Do you know what, Frenchman? Come on, I'll make way for you!' So the Englishman made way for the Frenchman.

The Miser

A miserly man had a profitable business in a small town. But everything was a little more expensive there, so he lived in a village half an hour away and walked in every morning and walked back in the evening. When a neighbour asked him for a favour, 'Would you be so kind and do this or that for me in town, it will save me the walk,' then he replied, 'It's bad enough having to wear out my shoe leather on my own business, do you expect me to do it on yours as well?' Then, if the neighbour said, 'You have to go anyway, whether you do me this little favour or not,' he replied, 'And if I don't, you'll have to use your own shoes to go to town, whether I go as well or not!' If then the neighbour said, 'Do you know what? I'll lend you my shoes!' he did him the favour. But if he didn't lend him his shoes he refused.

The Thief's Reply

A thief who gave himself airs was asked, 'Who do you think you are? You can't go back where you come from and should be glad that we put up with you here!' 'That's what you think!' said the thief, 'My masters back home are so fond of me that I know for certain if I went home they would never let me leave again.'

The Apprentice Boy

One day in Rheinfelden a young fellow caught thieving was put in the stocks, and all the time he was there, the iron collar round his neck, a well-dressed stranger stood among the lookers-on and never took his eyes off him. After an hour, when the thief was taken down from his place of honour to be given another twenty strokes to help him remember the occasion, this stranger went over to the constable, pressed a little thaler into his hand and said, 'Put a bit of effort into it, Lord help us! Let him have it for all you're worth!' And however hard the constable struck the thief the stranger yelled, 'Go to it! Harder still!' and in between he asked the young fellow on the whipping post with a malicious smile, 'How does that feel, my lad? How do you like that?'

But when the thief was run out of town the stranger followed him at a distance, caught up with him on the road to Degersfelden and said to him, 'Do you remember me, Gutschick?' The young fellow said, 'I won't forget you in a hurry! But tell me, why did you get so much enjoyment from my disgrace and the ticket of leave the constable wrote in big letters on my back? I didn't steal anything of yours or ever do anything to upset you!' The stranger said, 'It was a warning to you, because you did the job so stupidly you were bound to be caught! Those in our line of business – I'm Freddy Tinder,' he said, and so he was – 'Those in our line of business must start with cunning and finish with caution! But if you like you can come into apprenticeship with me, you're not short of intelligence it seems, and now you've had your warning, so I'll take you on and make something of you!' So he took the young fellow as his apprentice, and when it soon became unsafe by the Rhine he took him with him to the Spanish Netherlands.

The Snuffbox

There was quite a crowd at the inn in a village in the Netherlands, some knew each other, some didn't. It was market day, you see. No one knew Freddy Tinder. 'Another one for me too!' said a fat man in burgher's clothes to the landlord and took a pinch of snuff from a heavy silver snuffbox. Then Freddy Tinder saw how a skinny fellow in checks moved over to the fat man, started talking to him, and once or twice as if by chance glanced at his coat pocket where he had put the snuffbox. 'What's the betting,' thought Freddy, 'he's up to something?' At first the fellow stood, but then he had wine brought him and sat down on the bench too and started telling all sorts of funny stories that greatly amused the fat man. A little later a third fellow came up. 'Excuse me,' he said, 'could you make a bit of room?' So the skinny fellow wriggled up close to the fat man and went on telling his stories. 'Oh yes,' he said, 'I was really surprised when I came to this country and saw how the windmills turn so merrily in the wind all the time. Back home where I come from we never have a breath of wind all year round. So our windmills have to be built where the quails fly over. Then when in spring the quails come across the sea from Africa in their millions and fly over the windmills the sails start turning, and those who don't get their corn ground then have no flour for the rest of the year.' The fat man laughed so much he almost choked, and meanwhile the cunning fellow had taken the snuffbox. 'Give me a rest now!' said the fat man, 'my back's hurting,' and filled his glass for him. The rascal emptied the glass and said it was a good wine. 'It has a kick to it. Excuse me,' he said to the third fellow, who was nearer the door, 'I have to go outside a moment.' He had his hat on ready. But when he was outside the door and was making off, Freddy Tinder went into the yard after him, took him to one side and said, 'Hand over that silver snuffbox of my brother-in law's, will you? Do you think I didn't see you? Or shall I raise a hue and cry? I didn't want to say anything in front of the crowd inside.' As soon as the thief saw that he was caught he handed the box to Freddy, and he was trembling as he pleaded with him in God's name to keep quiet. 'Now you know,' said Freddy, 'what trouble you can land in if you leave the straight and narrow! Let it be a warning to last a lifetime. Ill-gotten wealth never prospers. Honesty is the best policy!' Freddy also had his hat on ready. So he gave the fellow another pinch of snuff from the box, and later took it to a goldsmith.

How Freddy Tinder Got Himself a Horse to Ride

At one time Freddy Tinder had performed nearly all the tricks a cunning thief can get up to and had almost tired of the business, for Freddy Tinder doesn't steal because he has to, nor for the sake of profit or from sheer wickedness, but for love of his craft and to sharpen his wits – don't you remember how he left the grey tied up at the miller of Brassenheim's door? What more could you, good reader, or Your Family Friend's companion on the road to Lenzkirch ask of him? One evening when, as said, he had run almost the whole gamut of tricks, he thought, 'Now for once I'll see how far you can get with honesty!' So that night he stole a goat three yards away from the constable on his beat and got himself caught. The next day at the hearing he confessed everything. But he quickly saw that the magistrate was going to give him five and twenty or something like that to remember him by, so he thought, 'I haven't been honest enough!' So he made one or two unwise remarks, and on further interrogation he confessed after initial resistance that he was born half albino, that meant that his eyes worked almost better in the dark than in daylight, and when the magistrate thought he could get the better of him and asked whether he couldn't recall a couple of other recent thefts, he said of course he remembered, he did them. The next morning when he was told the verdict, it was jail, and a soldier from the town guard was waiting by the door to escort him there, for the prison was twenty hours away, he said very contritely, 'Justice will be done. I deserve what's coming to me.'

On the road he told his escort he had been a soldier too. 'Six years I served with the Klebeck infantry. I could show you the seven wounds I got in the war on the Scheldt that the Emperor Joseph was out to wage with the Dutch, don't you know?' His simple-minded escort said, 'I never advanced beyond the town guard. I should have been a nail-maker but times are bad.' 'You've got it wrong,' said Freddy, 'a town soldier deserves more respect than a soldier in the field! For town comes before country, so that a soldier in the field can still advance to become a town soldier when he gets older. Besides, the town guard watches over his fellow citizens' lives and property and his own wife and children. The soldier who goes off to war doesn't know what or who he is fighting for. And besides,' he said, 'the town guard can, if he behaves himself, die with honour just as it suits him. For that the likes of us have to let themselves be cut to pieces. Take my word for it,' he went on, 'it does me and my enemies' (he meant the sheriff's men) 'no honour that I'm still alive.' The nail-maker was so touched by this flattering comparison that he thought to himself he couldn't recall ever

having conveyed such a kind-hearted and understanding prisoner. Meanwhile Freddy was striding ahead so as to make the nail-maker tired and thirsty in the heat of the sun. 'That's the difference between us in the field and you town guards,' he said, 'we are used to stretching our legs on the march.'

That afternoon at four o'clock they came to a village with an inn. 'How about a drink, comrade?' said Freddy. 'If you say so, comrade,' replied the nail-maker, 'I'll join you!' So they drank a glass of wine together, half a pint, then a pint, a quart, then two, and pledged to be bosom friends and brothers, and Freddy went on telling of his efforts in the war until the nail-maker fell asleep from wine and exhaustion. When he woke a few hours later and Freddy wasn't there, his first thought was, 'My new friend must have gone on slowly ahead!' But no, he was standing just outside the door, for Freddy doesn't leave empty handed. He came back in and said, 'Brother, the moon will soon be up. Don't you think we'd do better to stay here the night?' The sleepy nail-maker said wearily, 'If you say so!' That night the nail-maker slept soundly and snored all up the scale from bass to descant and down again, but Freddy couldn't sleep. He got up and whiled away the time searching through his new brother's pockets, and among other things he found the note about him that his escort was to give the governor of the jail. Then he whiled away the time trying on his brother's new regimental boots. They fitted him fine. Then, just to while away the time, he slipped through the window into the street and kept on straight down the road for as long as the moon lit his way.

When the nail-maker woke in the morning, and Freddy wasn't there, he thought, 'He'll be outside again.' Of course he had gone outside, and he walked on until the sun was up and then woke the mayor in the first village he came to. 'Mr Mayor, something awful's happened to me! I'm under arrest and I've lost the town guard who was supposed to escort me. I've got no money and don't know my way around these parts, so let me have something to eat on the parish and get someone to show me the way to the town and the jail.' The mayor wrote him a chitty for a bowl of soup and a glass of wine at the inn and sent for a girl. 'Go to the inn,' he told her, 'and when he's finished show the man having his breakfast there the way to town. He wants to go to the jail.'

When Freddy and the girl came out of the forest and over the last hills and he could see the towers of the town far away on the plain he said to her, 'You can go home now, my child, I can't go wrong now.' At the first houses in town he asked a small boy in the street, 'Boy, where's the jail?' And when he had found it and was admitted to the governor he gave him the note he had found in the nail-maker's pocket. The governor read it once, then again, and looked at Freddy in surprise. 'That's in order, my friend,' he said. 'But where's your prisoner? You are supposed to hand over a prisoner!' Freddy was taken aback and answered, 'Why, I'm the prisoner!' The governor said, 'It seems, my good friend, that you are having me on! We don't play jokes here. Own up, you let your prisoner escape! The signs are clear enough!' Freddy said, 'If you say the signs are clear then it's not for me to contradict. But if, Your Excellency,' he said to the governor, 'you let me have a man on horseback, I'm certain I can still catch the vagabond. It's hardly a quarter of an hour since he disappeared from my sight.' 'You idiot!' said the governor. 'What use is a fast horse if its rider has to take someone on foot with him? Can you ride?' Freddy said, 'I was with the Württemberg Dragoons for six years, you know!' 'Good,' replied the governor, 'We'll saddle up a mount for you as well, but you'll pay for it from your wages, mind! Next time pay more attention!' And he hurried to give him an open letter to the authorities in all the villages in case he needed men to make up a posse. So the constable and Freddy Tinder rode along together looking for Freddy Tinder, until they came to a crossroads. At the crossroads Freddy told the constable which way he was to go and which way he would go himself. 'We'll meet up at the Rhine by the ferry!' But when they were out of sight of each other Freddy turned to the right again and caused a commotion in all the villages with his letter and had them ring the alarm bells to warn that Freddy Tinder was in the area, until he came to the frontier. At the frontier he gave his horse a kick and rode across. Nothing like that could happen hereabouts!

The Champion Swimmer

Before the war and all its afflictions when you could still cross
freely from France to England and drink a glass or two in Dover
or buy material for a waistcoat, a large mail boat sailed from Calais
across the straits to Dover and back again twice a week. For the
sea between those two countries is only a few miles wide at that
point, you see. But you had to get there before the boat left if you
wanted to sail on it. A Frenchman from Gascony seemed not to
know that, for he came to Calais a quarter of an hour too late, just
as they were shutting up the hens, and the sky was clouding over.
'Must I sit around here for a couple of days twiddling my thumbs?
No,' he thought, 'I'd do better to pay a boatman a twelve-sous
piece to go after the mail boat.' For a small craft can sail faster
than the heavy mail boat, you understand, and will catch up with
it. But when he was sitting in the open boat the boatman said,
'If I'd thought I'd have brought a tarpaulin!' For it began to rain,
and how! Very soon it poured down from the night sky as if a sea
up above was emptying itself into the sea below. But the Gascon
thought, 'This is going to be fun!' 'Praise be,' said the boatman at
last, 'I can see the mail boat.' And he pulled up alongside and the
Gascon climbed aboard, and when he suddenly appeared
through the narrow hatchway in the middle of the night and in
the middle of the sea and joined the passengers on the ship they
all wondered where he had sprung from, all on his own, so late
and so wet. For on a ship like that it is like being in a cellar, you
can't hear what is going on outside over the talk of the passengers,
the sailors' shouts, the noise of the wind, the flapping sails and the
crashing waves, and nobody had any idea it was raining. 'You look
as if you've been keelhauled,' said one, 'pulled right under the

ship from one side to the other, I mean.' 'Is that what you're thinking?' said the Gascon. 'Do you imagine you can go swimming and stay dry? If you can tell me how to do that I'll be glad to hear it, you see I'm the postman from Oléron and every Monday I swim over to the mainland with letters and messages, it's quicker that way. But now I have a message to take to England. With your permission I'll join you, since I was fortunate enough to meet up with you. Judging from the stars it can't be far to Dover now.' 'You're welcome, fellow countryman,' said one (though he wasn't a fellow Frenchman but an Englishman) and blew a cloud of tobacco smoke from his mouth. 'If you have swum this far across the sea from Calais you must be a class above the black swimmer in London!' 'I'm not afraid of competition,' said the Gascon. 'Will you take him on,' replied the Englishman, 'if I place a hundred louis d'or on you?' The Gascon said, 'You can bet I will!' It's the custom of rich Englishmen to bet with each other for large sums placed on men who excel at some physical activity. And so it was that this Englishman on the ship took the Gascon to London with him at his expense and had him eat and drink well so that he stayed fit and strong. 'My lord,' he said to a good friend of his in London, 'I have brought with me a swimmer I found at sea. I bet you a hundred guineas he can beat your Moor!' His friend said, 'You're on!'

The next day they both appeared with their swimmers at an agreed spot on the river Thames, and hundreds of curious people had gathered there and they laid their bets too, some on the Moor, some on the Gascon, one shilling, or six shillings, one, two, five, twenty guineas, and the Moor didn't give the Gascon much of a chance. But when they had both undressed the Gascon tied a little box to his body with a leather strap without saying why, as if that were quite normal. The Moor said, 'What are you up to?

Have you learnt that from the champion jumper who had to tie lead weights to his feet when he was set to catch a hare and was afraid he would jump right over it?' The Gascon opened his box and said, 'I've only got a bottle of wine in here, a couple of saveloys and a small loaf of bread! I was going to ask you where you have your eats. For I shall swim straight down the river Thames into the North Sea and down the Channel into the Atlantic and on to Cadiz, and I suggest we don't call in anywhere on the way, for I have to be back in Oléron by Monday, that's the 16th. But tomorrow morning in Cadiz at the White Horse I'll order a good dinner for you so it will be ready by the time you arrive.' You, good reader, will hardly be imagining that he could escape that way! But the Moor was scared stiff. 'I can't compete against that amphibian!' he told his master. 'You can please yourself what you do!' And he got dressed again.

So the bet was over, the Gascon was given a handsome reward by the Englishman who had brought him there and everyone scoffed at the Moor. For although they must have seen that the Frenchman was only shamming, they were all amused by his bravado and the unexpected outcome, and for a month after that he was treated in the inns and beerhouses by all those who had bet on him, and he admitted he had never been in the water in all his life.

How a Fine Horse was Offered for Sale for Five of the Best

The following true story happened, if not in Salzwedel, then somewhere else, and Your Family Friend has it here in writing.

A cavalry officer, a captain, came into an inn. A customer there saw him dismount, he was a Jew, and said, 'That's a splendid sorrel Your Honour was riding.'

'You like the look of him then, Son of Jacob?' asked the officer.

'Not half! I'd put up with a hundred lashes just to lay hands on him!' replied the Jew.

The officer was tapping his whip against his boots. 'Why a hundred?' he said, 'You can have him for fifty.'

The Jew said, 'How about twenty-five?' 'Twenty-five would do,' said the officer, 'or fifteen, or five if you like!'

There was no telling whether he was joking or not. But when the officer said, 'Five would do, if you ask me,' the Jew thought, 'I put up with ten regulation strokes outside the courthouse at Günzburg, and I'm still kosher!' 'Sir,' he said, 'you're an officer. Officer's word of honour?' The captain said, 'Don't you trust my word? Do you want it in writing?'

'I'd prefer it that way,' said the Jew.

So the officer called a notary and had him draw up a deed for the Jew as follows: 'If the bearer of this deed endures five good strokes from a trusty stick applied by the gentleman officer present the aforesaid officer shall without further dues and demands give to him the bearer to be his property the sorrel saddle-horse at present in the keeping of the officer aforesaid. Made this day and at this place by the undersigned.'

When the Jew had put this document in his pocket he lay over a chair and the officer gave him such a hearty whack with a cane across his posterior that the Jew thought, 'He's a better hand at this than the constable in Günzburg!' and cried Ow! out loud, though he had determined not to utter a squeak.

But now the officer sat down and calmly drank a glass of wine. 'How do you like it, Jacob's son?' he asked. The Jew said, 'Never mind that, get on with it, let's have it over and done with!'

'My pleasure,' said the officer and gave him number two, and the first now seemed only an appetiser in comparison, then he sat down again and had another drink.

The third stroke was given in the same way, and the fourth. After the fourth the Jew said, 'I'm not sure if I should be grateful to Your Honour or not for allowing me time to relish each one separately. Now just give me number five to follow the fourth, then my happiness will be complete and the sorrel will know who to follow.'

Then the officer said, 'Jacob's son, you'll have to wait a long time for number five!' and he calmly put the cane back where he had found it, and all the begging and imploring for the fifth stroke was to no avail.

Now all those in the inn laughed until the house rocked on its foundations, but the Jew turned to the notary to help him get his fifth stroke and flourished the deed. But the notary said, 'Jacobson, what am I supposed to do with that? If the captain won't do it there's nothing in the deed to say he must.' So the Jew is still waiting to take receipt of the fifth stroke and the sorrel.

Your Family Friend would not find anything to admire in this trick if the Jew had not laid himself open to it.

Remember: A man who offers to take five of the best for profit deserves to get four of the best and gain nothing. You must never let yourself be abused for gain.

Franziska

In an insignificant little village on the Rhine, one evening just before nightfall a poor young weaver was still sitting at his loom, and as he worked he was thinking among other things of King

Hezekiah,* and then of his father and mother, the threads of whose lives too had been spun till the bobbin was empty, and then of his grandfather on whose knees he had sat and whom he had accompanied to his grave; and he was so lost in his thoughts and his work that he didn't notice a fine coach with four proud white horses come up to the house and draw to a halt. But when the latch opened and a young woman came in, a lovely creature with beautiful flowing hair and a long sky-blue dress, and she smiled a gentle smile and said in a soft voice, 'Do you remember me, Henry?' it was as if he woke with a start from a deep sleep, he was too amazed to speak. For he thought it was an angel, and he wasn't too far wrong, for it was his sister Franziska, and she was still alive.

Many a time once they had gone together barefoot collecting firewood in their baskets, many a Sunday they had picked

strawberries together and taken them to town, and eaten a piece
of bread on their way home and each took less so that the other
should have enough. But after their father died and poverty
drove her two brothers to leave home in search of work
Franziska stayed behind with her old ailing mother and looked
after her, earned a little money in a spinning mill to keep her, sat
up with her during the long sleepless nights and read to her
from an old tattered book about Holland, the beautiful houses
there, the great ships, and the dreadful battle of Dogger Bank,*
and she bore the whims of the sick old woman with the patience
of a child. But one night at two in the morning her mother said,
'Pray with me, daughter! I shall not see the light of day again in
this world.' Then the poor child prayed and sobbed and kissed
her dying mother, and her mother said, 'God bless you and' –
and she took the last part of her maternal blessing, 'and reward
you!' with her to eternity. When she was buried, Franziska
returned to the empty house and prayed and wept and
wondered what was to become of her now, and something
within her said, 'Go to Holland!' Slowly she raised her head and
looked up pensively, and for the time being no more tears
welled from her blue eyes. She made her way, praying and
asking alms and trusting in God, from village to town and town
to village till she reached Holland, and she had collected enough
to buy a decent dress. And as she was walking alone and lonely
through the busy streets of Rotterdam, again something within
her said, 'Go into that house there with the gilded bars at the
window!' She went through the entrance past the marble
stairway and through into the yard, for she hoped to meet
somebody there before she had to knock at a door – and there in
the yard stood a distinguished and kindly looking old lady
feeding the hens and doves and peacocks.

'What are you doing here, my child?' Franziska sensed she could trust this kind lady and told her her whole story. 'I'm a poor fledgeling who needs your hand to feed me,' said Franziska and asked for employment in her house. The lady felt she could trust the girl's modesty and innocence and the tears in her eyes, and she said, 'Don't worry, my child, God will not fail to honour your mother's blessing! I'll give you a position in my house and see that you are looked after if you are good.' For the woman was thinking, 'Who knows, it may be the good Lord's will that I should reward her', and she was a rich Rotterdam merchant's widow, though an Englishwoman by birth. So Franziska became a kitchen maid and then, when she proved a good faithful servant, she became parlour maid, and her mistress grew fond of her. And she showed good sense and learnt to fit in with refined ways and was employed as lady's maid. But that wasn't all.

In the spring when the roses came into flower one of the distinguished lady's relatives, a young Englishman, came from Genoa to visit her in Rotterdam. He came most years at this time, and as they talked about this and that and the young man was saying what it was like when the French had stood in the narrow Bochetta pass outside Genoa with the Austrians facing them,* Franziska came into the room with a happy smile and all the charm of youth and innocence to tidy something away – and when he saw her the Englishman's heart missed a beat and he forgot all about the French and the Austrians. 'Aunt,' he said, 'that girl you have as your lady's maid is as pretty as a picture! It's a pity she is not something better.' The aunt said, 'She is a poor orphan from Germany. She is not just pretty but also sensible, but more than that she is pious and virtuous, and I have come to love her as a daughter.' Her nephew thought that sounded encouraging.

Then, the next morning or the morning after that when he was walking with his aunt in the garden, she asked, 'What do you think of this rose?' He said, 'She's beautiful, very beautiful!' The aunt said, 'Nephew, you're talking nonsense! Who's beautiful? I was speaking of this rose.' He said, 'I meant the rose!' 'Not Franziska then?' asked his aunt. 'I'm not blind!' she said. The nephew confessed that he loved the girl and would like to marry her. The aunt said, 'Nephew, you shall stay here another three weeks. If you still feel the same then, I have no objections. The girl deserves a good husband.' Then after three weeks he said, 'It's worse now and I don't know how I could live without the girl!' So they were engaged. Though much persuasion was needed to overcome the pious girl's humility.

She stayed another year with the woman who had been her mistress in the fine house with the gilded bars at the window, no longer as lady's maid now but as friend and relative, and during this time she learnt English and French and to play the piano. 'When we are in trouble sore', 'The Lord who all things doth rule', 'In you, dear Lord, my trust I place', these and other things she learnt that a lady's maid has no cause to know but a fine lady should. The groom returned a few weeks before the year was out and the wedding was celebrated in the aunt's house. But when talk turned to the newly married couple leaving, the young wife looked beseechingly at her husband and asked that she might return to her beloved homeland again and visit her mother's grave and thank her, and she would also like to see her brothers again and her friends.

So it was that she paid a visit that evening on her brother, the poor weaver, and when he did not reply to her question, 'Do you remember me, Henry?', she said, 'I'm your sister Franziska.' In his surprise he dropped the shuttle on the floor, and his sister embraced him. Yet at first his joy was somewhat muted, for she was now a great lady and he was embarrassed that the foreign gentleman, her husband, should see poverty and riches embracing like brother and sister and on familiar terms with each other, until he saw that though she no longer wore the dress of poverty she was still clothed in humility, her position had changed, but not her heart. A few days later, after she had visited all her relatives and acquaintances, she left with her husband for Genoa, and they are probably living in England now, where some time later her husband inherited a rich estate.

Your Family Friend will be honest and confess what moves him most in this story. He is most moved because the good Lord was present when the dying mother blessed her daughter and He called a merchant's lady in Rotterdam in Holland and a good rich Englishman by the sea in Italy to fulfil a poor dying widow's blessing on her pious child.

'Thou everywhere hast sway,
And all things serve Thy might.'

Married on Sentry Duty

At two o'clock one night without warning a regiment that had been stationed in a village for six weeks was suddenly given orders to break camp at once. So at three o'clock they were all on the march, except for a lone sentry out in the fields who had been forgotten in the hurry and remained where he was. At first time did not drag for this soldier alone at his sentry post. For he gazed at the stars and thought, 'You can twinkle as long as you like, you're not a patch on those two eyes that are sleeping now down at the bottom mill!' Yet towards five o'clock he thought, 'It must be getting on for three.' But no one came to relieve him. The quails called, the village cock crowed, the last stars had disappeared, promising to return that next night, the day stirred into life, men came into the fields, but our musketeer still stood at his post waiting to be relieved. Eventually a farmer out on his field told him that the whole battalion had marched away at three o'clock, there was not a gaiter strap left in the village, let alone its owner. So the musketeer took matters in his own hands and went back to the village without being relieved. He ought to have marched after his regiment at the double. But this musketeer thought, 'If they don't need me any more, I can manage without them.' He also thought, 'It's no bad thing. If I go to find them without orders and without being relieved I could find myself exposed to a storm of falling sticks.' Besides, he thought, 'The bottom miller has a pretty daughter, and she has a pretty mouth and her mouth lovely kisses,' and if anything else had happened by then that's none of our business. So he took off his blue tunic and found work on a farm in the village, and if anyone asked he gave an answer that's been given by others, he said he had had bad luck and lost his regiment. He was a willing hand, quick and efficient at his work and good-looking too. He was poor of course, but that only made the miller's daughter a suitable match, for the miller had a few pennies. So they were married. The young couple lived together in loving harmony and set up their little home. But one day after a year had passed he came home from the fields and his wife met him with a worried look on her face. 'Freddy, we had a visit that won't please you.' 'Who was it?' 'The billeting officer from your regiment. They'll be here in an hour!' The old miller was desolated, his daughter was desolated and looked at the baby at her breast with tears in her eyes. For someone was bound to tell on him. But after the first shock

Freddy said, 'Leave it to me! I know the colonel.' So he put on his blue tunic again that he had meant to keep as a souvenir, and told his father-in-law what to do. Then he shouldered his musket and went back to his post. And when the battalion had marched in the old miller appeared before the colonel. 'Have a thought, general, for the poor fellow who was put on sentry duty a year ago out there at the corner of the wood. Are you supposed to leave a sentry at his post for a whole year without relieving him?' The colonel looked at the captain, the captain looked at the sergeant, the sergeant at the corporal, and half the company, who knew the missing man well, ran out to see the year-old sentry and how he must be shrivelled up out there like a prune left too long in the sun. Eventually the corporal, the one who had placed him at his post twelve months before, came and relieved him: 'Present arms! Shoulder arms! Quick march!' according to military rules and tradition. He was taken before the colonel, and his pretty young wife went with him with her baby in her arms and they had to tell him everything. But the colonel was a kindly man and gave him a thaler and helped him get his discharge.

Two Honest Tradesmen

Two broom-makers were selling their wares next to each other in Hamburg. When one of them had sold nearly all his brooms, the other, who had sold none at all, said to his neighbour, 'I just don't understand it, mate, how can you sell your brooms so cheaply? I steal the twigs for mine too and yet can scarcely make ends meet.' 'I can believe that, mate,' came the reply, 'I steal mine ready made.'

Cunning Meets its Match

Two elegantly dressed individuals had bought 3,000 thalers' worth of precious jewellery from a well-known goldsmith for the coronation in Hungary. They put down 1,000 thalers in cash, packed all the pieces they had chosen into a casket, sealed it and left it with him, as a pledge so to speak until they paid the full amount; at least that is how it seemed to the goldsmith. 'We'll be back with the money in a fortnight,' they said, 'and collect the casket.' It was all put down in writing. But three weeks went by and they didn't come back. The coronation day passed, and another four weeks. They weren't likely to come for the casket now. In the end the goldsmith thought, 'Why should I look after their property at my risk and let my capital lie idle?' So he had the casket opened in the presence of an official and proposed depositing with the authorities the 1,000 thalers he had received.

But when the casket was opened the lawyer said, 'My dear goldsmith, I'm afraid you've been hoodwinked by those two rascals all right!' For it contained pebbles instead of gems and glazing lead instead of gold. The two buyers were a couple of rascally conjurors, Bohemian Jews, the goldsmith hadn't noticed, but they had replaced the real casket with another one that looked just like it. 'There's nothing we can do about it now,' said the lawyer. 'It's bad luck, I'm afraid!' At that moment another stranger, well-dressed and honourable in manner, came in the door wanting to sell the goldsmith a collection of bent silver tableware and odd buckles, and saw what was going on. 'Goldsmith,' he said when the lawyer was gone, 'never have anything to do with pen-pushers! Stick to practical people. Help is at hand if you have the courage to cast a sprat to catch a mackerel! If your casket or the money they got for it still exists I'll lure the rascals back into your house.' 'Who may you be, if I might ask?' said the goldsmith. 'I'm Freddy Tinder,' replied the stranger confidently, with the friendly smile of a likeable rogue. If you don't know Freddy personally, as Your Family Friend does, you cannot imagine how honest and good-natured he can appear, and how he can capture the heart and trust of even the most cautious of men, just like their money! Besides, he's really not so bad as people the length of Germany think. Maybe the goldsmith also thought of the saying that poachers make the best gamekeepers, or perhaps of another saying, in for a penny, in for a pound. However it was, he decided to trust Freddy. 'But don't let me down, I beg you,' he said. 'Just rely on me,' said Freddy. 'And don't be too surprised if you have learnt another lesson by tomorrow morning!'

Are you thinking Freddy is already hot on the scent? No, not yet! But that same night someone came to the goldsmith's house and took four dozen silver spoons, six dozen silver salt-cellars, six gold rings with precious stones, and that someone was Freddy! Some of you who don't care too much about the goldsmith will be thinking, 'Serves him right!' There's no harm in that. He didn't mind, you see! For on the table he found a receipt in Freddy Tinder's own hand, acknowledging that he had taken delivery of the said items, and a note telling him what to do. So, as Freddy instructed, the goldsmith reported the theft and requested an on-the-spot investigation. Then he asked the sheriff's officer to put a complete list of the stolen articles in all the newpapers. And he asked that the sealed casket should, for a consideration, be described in every detail in that list. The officer saw his way clear and agreed to his request. 'A man with a family to keep can do an honest goldsmith a favour,' he thought. So all the papers reported that the goldsmith had had such and such stolen, among other things a casket answering to such and such a description, containing many precious gems, all listed. The news reached Augsburg. 'Loeb,' smirked one Bohemian Jew to the other, 'that goldsmith will never find out what was in that casket! Have you heard it's been stolen from him?' 'That's a stroke of luck,' said Loeb, 'now he will have to give us our money back and he'll be left with nothing!' They had fallen into Freddy's trap, and went back to the goldsmith's.

'We've come for our casket. You remember, we've kept you waiting a little while.' 'My dear sirs,' said the goldsmith, 'a disaster has happened, your casket has been stolen! Didn't you see it in the papers?' Loeb replied calmly, 'We are sorry, but surely the misfortune is yours! Either give us the casket we left in your keeping, or return our deposit! The coronation is over anyway.' They exchanged a word or two, and the goldsmith said, 'The misfortune is yours, I tell you!' For at that moment his wife came into the room with four sheriff's men, sturdy fellows all as such men are, and they took hold of the rogues. The casket was never traced, but they did find a prison cell big enough for two, and enough in money and in kind to pay the goldsmith. In gratitude he tore up Freddy's receipt. But Freddy returned everything and asked no payment for his help. 'If I ever need anything of yours again,' he said, 'I know my way to your shop and the strong box! I just wish I could ruin all the rascals,' he said, 'so that I was the only one left!' For he's jealous of rivals, you see.

A Willing Justice

During the republic* a newly appointed magistrate was on the bench for the first time when the miller from the bottom mill appeared before him to put a complaint against the top miller over river maintenance costs. When he had stated his case the magistrate acknowledged, 'The matter is very clear! You are in the right.' One night and a few drinks passed, then the miller from the top mill appeared and defended himself and demanded justice even more volubly. When he had finished speaking the magistrate acknowledged, 'The case couldn't be clearer! You are completely in the right.' The miller left the room, then the clerk came up to the bench. 'Your Honour,' said the clerk, 'your predecessor never, all the time he sat on the bench, acted like this while administering justice. And we can't go on like this. Both parties can't win a case, or else they must both also lose, and that won't work!' Now the magistrate answered, 'No case has ever been clearer! You are right too.'

Pious Advice

An eighteen-year-old lad, inexperienced, Catholic and pious, left his parents' home for the first time to go on his travels. At the first large town he paused on the bridge to look around him to right and left, for he feared he wouldn't see too many bridges like this one again with houses built above and below it. But when he looked to the right a priest was coming towards him from that side, carrying that hallowed article before which every humble and sincere Catholic falls to his knees. When he looked round to

the left another priest was coming from the other end of the bridge, and he too was carrying that hallowed article before which every humble and sincere Catholic falls to his knees, and both were quite close to him and about to pass him at the same time, the one approaching from this side on his left, the other from that side on his right. Now the poor fellow didn't know which way to turn, whether to kneel to this hallowed article or to that one, and to which one he should direct his prayer and his devotion, and there was no easy answer. But when in his distress he looked at one of the priests and his look asked what he should do, the priest smiled like a kind angel at this pious soul and raised his hand and pointed a finger towards the light in the heavens high above. He meant, you see, he was to kneel to Him above and worship Him. Your Family Friend can respect and applaud that advice even if he has never told a rosary – if he had he wouldn't be writing the Lutheran calendar.

The Weather Man

Just as a sieve-maker or a basket-weaver who lives in a small place cannot earn enough in his village or town to keep himself all year, but has to look for work and practise his craft in the countryside around, so our compasses-maker too does business away from home, and his trade is not in compasses but in knavish tricks that pay for a few drinks at the inn. Thus one day he appeared in Oberehingen and went straight to the mayor. 'Mr Mayor,' he said, 'could you do with different weather? I've seen how things are hereabouts. There's been too much rain on the bottom fields and the crops on the hill are behindhand.' The mayor thought that was easy to say but difficult to put right. 'Just so,' replied the compasses-maker, 'but that's my line of business! Didn't you know I'm the weather man from Bologna?' In Italy, he said, where the oranges and lemons grow, all the weather was made to order. 'You Germans are a bit behind in these matters.' The mayor was a good and trusting fellow and one of those who would like to get rich sooner rather than later. So he was attracted by the offer. But he also thought caution was called for! 'As a test run,' he said, 'make it a clear sky tomorrow with just a few fluffy white clouds, sunshine all day with some streaks of vapour glistening in the air. Let the first yellow butterflies come out round midday, and it can be a nice cool evening!' The compasses-maker replied, 'I can't commit myself just for one day, Mr Mayor! It wouldn't cover my costs. I can only take on the job by the year. But then you'll have problems finding room to store your crops and the new wine!' When the mayor wanted to know how much he would charge for the year he was careful and didn't ask for payment in advance, only a guilder a day and free drinks until the matter was properly in hand, that could take at least three days – 'But after that a pint from each gallon of wine over what you press in your best years, and a peck from every bushel of fruit.' 'That's risnible,' said the mayor. He stood in awe of the compasses-maker and was using refined language, and people in his part of the country think it's refined to say 'risnible' for reasonable. But when he took pen and paper from the cupboard and was drawing up a schedule for the weather month by month the compasses-maker came up with a further complication: 'You can't do that, Mr Mayor! You will have to consult the people. The weather is a community matter. You can't expect everyone to accept your choice of weather.' 'You're right!' said the mayor. 'You're a sensible man.'

You, good reader, will have taken the measure of our compasses-maker and will have foreseen that the people could not agree on the matter. At their first meeting no decision was reached, nor even at the seventh, at the eighth hard words were spoken, and in the end a level-headed lawyer concluded that the best thing to do, to preserve peace and avoid strife in the community, was to pay the weather man off and send him packing. So the mayor summoned the compasses-maker. 'Here are your nine guilders, you mischief-maker, now make sure you leave before there's blood shed in the village!' The compasses-maker didn't have to be told twice. He took the money, left owing for about twelve pints of wine at the inn, and the weather stayed as it was.

Now then, as always the compasses-maker has much to teach us! In this case how good it is that up till now the supreme ruler of the world has always governed the weather according to his will alone. Even we calendar-makers, luminaries and the other estates of the realm are scarcely consulted and need lose no sleep on that score.

The Tailor at Penza

An honest calendar man, Your Family Friend for instance, has been given an important and enjoyable task by the Lord God, that is to show how eternal providence provides help before the need is too great, and to proclaim the praise of excellent men wherever they may be.

This tailor in Penza, what a splendid little fellow he was! Twenty-six journeymen under him, year in, year out, enough work for half of Russia, and yet no money, but a happy, joyful disposition, a heart worth more than its weight in gold, and German blood and Rhenish hospitality in the middle of Asia!

In 1812 when there weren't enough roads in Russia for the prisoners of war taken by the Beresina or at Vilna,* one of those roads went through Penza, which is more than one hundred days' journey from Lahr or Pforzheim and where the best German or English watch, if you have one, doesn't show the right time but is always a few hours slow. Penza is the residence of the first Russian governor in Asia as you leave Europe. The prisoners of war were handed over there before being sent further into the depths of alien Asia where Christianity stops and no one knows the Lord's Prayer unless he brings it with him as a foreign ware from Europe. So one day there arrived in Penza, along with French prisoners, sixteen officers from the Rhineland* who had served under Napoleon's banners, they were weary from the battlefields and conflagrations of Europe, their limbs frozen and their wounds not properly healed, they were ill, without money, clothes or hope, and in that land they found nobody who understood their language or who pitied them in their plight. They looked at each other in despair. 'What shall become of us?'

they thought, or 'When will death end our misery and who will bury the last of us to die?' Then all of a sudden in the midst of the babble of Russians and Cossacks they heard, like the glad tidings sent from heaven, a voice saying, 'Any Germans there?' And there stood, though not on an equal footing, a very welcome friendly figure! It was the tailor at Penza, Franz Anton Egetmeier, born in Bretten in the Neckar district in the Grand Duchy of Baden. He learnt his trade in Mannheim in the year 1779, don't you know? Then he moved to Nuremberg and then on a bit to St Petersburg. A tailor from the Palatinate isn't afraid of seven to eight hundred hours on the road if the spirit moves him! In St Petersburg he took a job as regimental tailor in a Russian cavalry regiment, and he rode with them, wielding now his scissors and now his sword, into the strange Russian world where nothing is the same as here, and to Penza. Later he set up in civilian life in Penza and he is now a highly respected little fellow there. Anyone in Asia who wants a nice smart coat sends to the German tailor in Penza. The governor, a distinguished man who has the ear of the Tsar, grants him favours as to a friend; and if anyone up to thirty hours' journey away is in trouble he turns to the tailor in Penza and finds just what he needs, comfort, advice, help, a heart full of love, shelter, a meal and a bed, everything except money.

The battlefields of 1812 brought a wonderful harvest of joy to a heart like his, rich only in love and kindness. Whenever a batch of unfortunate prisoners arrived he threw down his scissors and his tape and was the first on the square, and his first question was, 'Any Germans there?' From one day to the next he hoped to find fellow countrymen among the prisoners and looked forward to helping them, and he loved them in anticipation before he had seen them, just as a woman loves her child and can feed it before she has it. 'If only they look like this or like that,' he thought. 'If only they are in great need so that I can be a great help to them!' But when there were no Germans he made do with Frenchmen and did all he could to lighten their misery before they were moved on. Yet this time there were fellow countrymen there, quite a few of them, from Darmstadt and other familiar places too, and when he shouted, 'Any Germans there?' he had to ask a second time, for at first they were too amazed and disbelieving to answer, the sweet sound of German in Asia rang in their ears like the sound of a harp. And when they replied, 'Quite a few of us Germans!' he asked them all where they came from. He would have been happy with Mecklenburg or the Electorate of Saxony, but one said, 'From Mannheim on the river Rhine!' as if the tailor didn't know where Mannheim was, another, 'From Bruchsal', a third, 'From Heidelberg', and a fourth, 'From Gochsheim', and the tailor's whole being glowed with happiness. 'And I come from Bretten!' said the splendid fellow Franz Anton Egetmeier from Bretten, just as Joseph said to the children of Israel in Egypt, 'I am your brother Joseph!' And tears of joy and sadness and of sacred love for the homeland welled in all their eyes, and it was difficult to say who was more glad and the more moved, they at finding him or he at finding them. Then the good man led his dear fellow countrymen in triumph to his house and to as good a meal as could be got together in a hurry.

Now he hurried to the governor and asked his gracious permission to keep the Germans in Penza. 'Anton,' said the governor, 'when did I refuse you anything?' So he ran round town to his friends and acquaintances in search of the best quarters for those for whom he had no space in his own home. He inspected his guests one by one. 'My friend,' he said to one, 'your linen looks the worse for wear. I'll find half a dozen new shirts for you.' 'You need a new tunic too,' he said to another. 'Yours can be turned and mended,' to another, and all of them were treated the same, and at once cloth was cut to size and all twenty-six journeymen worked day and night on clothes for his dear fellow countrymen from the Rhine. In a few days they were all fitted out with new or decent things. Even in an hour of need a good man never takes advantage of a stranger's kindness; so his guests from the Rhineland said to him, 'You mustn't count on us. Prisoners of war have no money. And we don't know how we'll be able to repay you the great sums you have spent, or when.' But the tailor replied, 'I have sufficient reward if I can help you. Make use of everything I have, make yourselves at home!' Spoken like an emperor or a king, simple and offhand words, where kindness is clothed in dignity! For not only high princely birth and magnanimity, ordinary humble love too can quite spontaneously inspire the heart to regal words, not to speak of thoughts. He took them as happy as a child around the town and paraded them in front of his friends. We cannot record here all the good things he did for them. However happy they were, he was never satisfied. Every day he discovered new ways of lightening the pains of captivity and of making life pleasant for them in that strange place in Asia. When there was a royal birthday or nameday back home it was celebrated with a banquet, cheers and fireworks by these loyal subjects there in Asia, on the same day too, only a bit earlier, because the clocks are wrong there. When good news arrived of the allies' victorious advance in Germany, the tailor was the first to know and passed it on to his children – he now always called them his children – with tears of joy because it brought their release nearer. When the prisoners received money from home their first care was to repay their benefactor. 'My sons,' he said, 'don't spoil my pleasure!' 'Father Egetmeier,' they said, 'don't hurt our feelings!' So as not to offend them he presented them with a little bill and then spent the money on providing pleasures for them, down to the last copeck. The money had been meant for something else, but you can't think of everything. You see, when at last the day of their release arrived their boundless joy was mixed with bitter sorrow at parting, and this was joined by dire distress. For they lacked everything needed for such a long journey through the terrors of the Russian winter and an inhospitable land, and although they were each given thirteen kreuzers for each day they would travel across Russia, that wouldn't take them very far. So in those final days the tailor, otherwise so cheerful and carefree, went around in silence as if something was on his mind, and he was seldom at home. 'He's really upset,' said his Rhenish guests, but they didn't notice anything. But then he bounced in with joy in his stride and beamed and said, 'Friends, I've found a way! Plenty of money!' What do you think he had done? The good soul had sold his house for two thousand roubles! 'I'll find somewhere to live all right,' he said, 'just as long as you get back to Germany safe and sound.' Oh the holy words of the gospel and His love made flesh: 'Go and sell what thou hast, and give to the poor, and thou shalt have treasure in heaven.' He will be found above on the right hand when the voice has spoken, 'Come, ye blessed! I was an hungered and ye gave me meat, I was naked and ye clothed me, I was sick and in prison and ye ministered unto me.' But to the prisoners' great relief the sale was revoked. Nevertheless he found a way of getting a few hundred roubles for them and made them take all his valuable Russian furs with them so that they could sell them if they needed money or one of them needed special care on the journey. Your Family Friend will not attempt to describe their leave-taking. No one who was there could do that. Finally they parted with a thousand blessings and tears of gratitude and love, and the tailor confessed that this was the saddest day of his life. And on their journey back they never stopped talking about their father in Penza, and when they arrived safely in Bialystok in Poland and found money waiting for them there they returned with thanks the sum he had advanced for the journey.

And now you have heard about God's child Franz Anton Egetmeier, master tailor in Asia.

Tit For Tat

The vicar of Trudenbach was standing at his window one afternoon when he saw the Jew from Brassenheim passing by with his pack on his shoulder. 'Moses,' the vicar called out to him, 'if you find me a good buyer for my horse, it's worth twenty doubloons, there'll be something in it for you!' 'Well, and what will I get?' 'A sack of oats.' But three weeks passed before the Jew found the right buyer, one who paid six doubloons more for the horse than it was worth, and in the meantime the price of oats soon doubled because the French were buying it up everywhere, at that time they were still buying. So the vicar gave the Jew half a sack instead of a full one. 'Perhaps I'll convert him,' he thought, 'when he sees that we are fair in our dealings too.'

There was more than one way of taking that. But the Jew took it to be only right and proper. 'You wait, you goy,' he thought, 'you'll be needing me again!'

A year later the vicar of Trudenbach was standing at his

window and the Jew from Brassenheim was passing through the village. 'Moses,' the vicar called out to him, 'I have two fat oxen to sell. If you can find me . . .' 'Well, and what will I get if I find you a good buyer?' 'Two big thalers.'

The Jew went to see a bankrupt butcher who had not wielded a cleaver for some time, for all good things must come to an end – not paying bills, for instance. Eventually he told his last two customers, 'I don't know how it is, I've been so tender-hearted for some time now, I can't stand the sight of blood any more,' and he shut up shop. Since then he had a nickname, Butcher Bloodshy, and earned a living, like the compasses-maker, from little ruses and tricks – like this one now. For in him the Jew was looking for and found his man, and he told him what was to be had and how. Two days later they went off to see the vicar. And can you imagine how the butcher was rigged out? In a more or less new coat of brown cloth, long trousers of smart striped fustian, an empty money belt round his middle, a silver ring as heavy as lead on his finger, a similar heart on his shirt beneath a scarlet neckerchief, and a well-fed dog at his heels – all borrowed on the Jew's security, nothing that was his own except his red face! The oxen were walked round professionally, prodded and sized up, weighed and measured by eye. 'So how much are you asking for them?' 'Twenty doubloons.' 'Seventeen!' 'Make it nineteen, landlord,' said the Jew, 'you won't regret it!' 'They're fine oxen,' said Bloodshy. 'If I'd known two hours ago when my purse was full I'd have given a couple of doubloons more to get hands on them straight away. But I'll fetch them on Friday for eighteen.' And he pulled out his leather purse as if he was going to pay a deposit. The Jew had been whispering something in the vicar's ear. 'If you put down two big thalers so he can pay his cook,' he said to the butcher, 'you can take the oxen away now for nineteen. You're a man of honour and so is his Reverence the Dean. Bring him the money on Friday.' The sale was agreed, two big thalers changed hands. 'Landlord,' said the Jew, 'you've struck a good deal!'

So Bloodshy drove off the fine fat prizes. But (as most of you, good readers, will have guessed!) the Dean didn't get his money that Friday.

Four weeks later (or was it six?) the vicar of Trudenbach was standing at his window one afternoon and the Jew from Brassenheim was passing through the village. 'Moses,' the vicar called out to him, 'where's that landlord of yours? I still haven't got my money!' 'Where he is?' said Moses. 'He'll be waiting for a doubloon to double in value, then he'll bring you nine and a half instead of nineteen. Will you lose anything that way? Did I lose anything with my oats a year ago?'

The vicar saw the daylight then.

The nicest thing about this story is that it's true. The Jew afterwards told it himself and made much of how honestly the butcher went halves with him at the crossroads in the forest. 'You know what he did?' he said. 'He kept the best one for himself and gives me the other one.'

Mister Charles

A merchant in St Petersburg, a Frenchman by birth, was rocking his lovely baby boy on his knees and his expression said he was a wealthy and happy man who took his good fortune as a blessing from God. At that moment a stranger, a Pole, came into the room with four sickly and half frozen children. 'Here are the children!' he said. The merchant looked at the Pole in surprise.

'What am I meant to do with them? Whose children are they? Who sent you here?' 'They're nobody's now,' said the Pole, 'they belong to a woman dead in the snow, seventy hours down the road to Vilna. You can do what you like with them.' The merchant said, 'You must have come to the wrong place,' and Your Family Friend thinks he was right. But the Pole was not put out and answered, 'If you are Mister Charles I'm in the right place,' and Your Family Friend thinks he was right too. It was Mister Charles! You see, a Frenchwoman, a widow, had lived prosperous and blameless in Moscow for many years, but when, five years before, the French were in Moscow they treated her too much like one of them for the inhabitants' liking. For blood is thicker than water, and after she too had lost her home and her wealth in the great fire* and had saved only her five children she had to leave the city and the country as a suspected collaborator. Otherwise she would have gone to St Petersburg to look for her rich cousin. Now, good reader, you will be thinking things are beginning to add up! But she fled to Vilna through the terrible cold and suffered unspeakable hardships, lacking everything needed to make such a long trek bearable, and she fell ill, when in Vilna she met an excellent Russian prince and appealed to him for help. This excellent prince gave her three hundred roubles and, learning that she had a cousin in St Petersburg, let her choose between going on to France or official permission to go back to St Petersburg. She looked doubtfully at her eldest boy, for he was the most sensible and the most ill. 'Where do you want to go?' 'I'll go wherever you're going, mother,' said the boy, and he was right, for he was in his grave before they left. So she got things ready for the journey and arranged with a Pole to take her to her cousin in St Petersburg for five hundred roubles; for he will make up the sum, she thought. But with each day of the long difficult journey she became more ill, and she died on the sixth or seventh day.

'I'll go wherever you go,' the dead boy had said, and the Pole inherited the surviving children from her, and they were able to converse to the limits of what a Pole can understand when a French child speaks Russian or a little Frenchman when someone tries to speak to him in Polish. Not many of you, good readers, would have swapped places with him. He himself was far from happy. 'What shall I do?' he said to himself. 'Turn back? Where shall I leave the children? Go on? Who shall I take them to?' Do as conscience dictates, said something within him finally: would you rob the poor children of the only thing they can inherit from their mother, your word you gave her? So he knelt down with the unhappy orphans beside her body and said an Our Father in Polish with them. 'And lead us not into temptation!' Then they all threw a tiny handful of snow on their mother's cold breast and shed a farewell tear, they wanted to do their last duty by her at her burial as best they could, they were wretched orphans now. But as he drove with them along the road to St Petersburg he was easier in his mind for he couldn't imagine that He who had entrusted the children to him would forsake him. And eventually, when the great city was spread before him, like a hired driver who only asks where he is to stop when he has reached the edge of town, he asked the children, getting them to understand him as best he could, where their cousin lived, and learnt from them, as far as he could understand them, 'We don't know.' What was his name? 'We don't know.' What was their surname? 'Charles.' Now you will be thinking things are now adding up even more, and if Your Family Friend had his way Mister Charles would indeed be the cousin, the children would be provided for, and that would be the end of the story. But truth is often stranger than fiction. No, our Mister Charles was not their cousin, but another man of the same name, and to this day nobody knows the real cousin's name nor whether he was living in St Petersburg or elsewhere. So for two days the poor man went around the town in great perplexity, anxious to dispose of his load of little Frenchmen. But no one took it upon himself to ask, 'What do you want for two of them?' And now Mister Charles didn't even want them for nothing, at that moment he had no intention of keeping just one of them. But when one word led to another and the Pole told him in simple words their sad story, he thought, 'I'll take one off his hands,' and he felt a warm glow within his breast. 'I'll take two off his hands,' he thought, and when the children nestled around him thinking he was their cousin and began to weep in French (for you will of course have noticed that French children weep differently) Mister Charles saw what they meant in their foreign way, God touched his heart and he felt like a father whose own children are weeping and wailing. 'In God's name', he said, 'if this is how it is I'll not pretend it's no business of mine!' and he took delivery of the children. 'Sit down for a while,' he said to the Pole, 'I'll have some soup brought you.'

The Pole tucked into the soup with a good appetite and lighter heart, and put down his spoon. He put down his spoon but didn't get up, then he got up but stood where he was. 'Be so good,' he said at last, 'and settle with me, Vilna's a long way from here! The lady agreed on five hundred roubles.' Mister Charles was a mild man, but at this his face darkened like a sunny meadow in spring when a cloud passes over. 'I'm not sure I understand you, my friend,' he said. 'I'm taking the children off your hands, aren't you satisfied with that? Do you expect me to pay you carriage as well?' For it can happen to the most decent and best of men, and not just to merchants, that, without knowing or intending to, they have to begin by haggling a bit, even if it is only with themselves. The Pole answered, 'My good sir, I won't tell you now what I think of you! I've brought you the children, aren't you satisfied with that? Did you expect me to drive them here for nothing? Times are bad and money hard to come by!' 'Just so,' said Mister Charles, 'and that applies to me too. Or do you think I'm so rich that I buy up other people's children, or so wicked that I trade in them? Do you want them back?' Again one word led to another and the Pole now learnt to his astonishment that Mister Charles was not the cousin but was only taking in the poor children from pity. 'If that's the case,' he said, 'I'm not a rich man, and your countrymen, the French, haven't made me any richer either, but if that's how things are then I can't ask any more of you. Just treat the poor things kindly,' said the noble fellow, and a tear came into his eye as from a heart that was overwhelmed, certainly Mister Charles's heart was overwhelmed by it. 'Monsieur Charles,' he thought, 'and a poor Polish carrier!' And the Pole had already begun to kiss the children goodbye, urging them in Polish to be obedient and god-fearing, when Mister Charles said, 'Wait a moment, my friend! I'm not really so hard up that I can't pay you for the good job you did bringing this little load here now that I have accepted the consignment!' And he gave him the five hundred roubles. So now the children are provided for, the carrier has been paid, and if when we got to the city gates one or two of you, good readers, doubted whether the cousin could be found and whether he would play his part, you now see that divine providence did not even need him.

The Glove Merchant

A dealer who wanted to bring a crate of fine gloves from France over into Germany used the following ploy. There's a law, you see, that anyone bringing goods into or out of France has to declare their value at the French customs post. If he declares them at a reasonable value, good, then he pays the duty, it's so much or just that. But if the customs officer sees that a merchant or shopkeeper has named much too low a price so as to pay too little duty, then that customs man can say, 'Very well, I'll give you that plus ten percent!' and then the merchant has to accept it. The tradesman gets the money and the officer gets the goods, and they are then auctioned in Colmar or Strassburg or some such town. It's a cunning scheme, you can't quarrel with it. But cunning can always be outdone! A merchant who wanted to bring two crates of gloves over the Rhine came to an understanding with a friend beforehand. Then he put only right-hand gloves, two by two, into one crate, and all the left-hand ones into another crate. The left-hand gloves he smuggled over on a misty night. What the eye doesn't see the heart doesn't grieve over! He arrived at the customs post with the others. 'What's in that crate?' 'Gloves from Paris.' 'Their value?' 'Two hundred francs.' The customs man felt the gloves. The leather was soft, it was strong too, the stitches were finely sewn, clearly they were worth four hundred francs of anyone's money. 'I'll give you two hundred and twenty francs for them,' said the customs man, 'Hand them over!' The dealer said, 'You've made an offer I can't resist.' Ten percent is a profit after all! So he pocketed two hundred and twenty francs and abandoned the crate. The next Friday the gloves were offered at auction in the market hall in Speyer, at that time under

the French. 'Who will bid me more than two hundred and
twenty?' The interested parties inspected the gloves. 'It seems to
me,' said the dealer's friend, 'that we're a little short on left ones.'
'Parbleu!' said someone else, 'they're all right-hand gloves!'
Nobody made a bid. 'Two hundred, anyone? One hundred and
fifty? One hundred? Eighty, anyone?' Nobody made a bid. 'You
know something?' said the dealer's friend eventually, 'perhaps a
lot of one-armed men will return from the war.' It was in the year
1813. 'I'll give sixty francs for them,' he said. And they were
knocked down to him. As for the customs officer from over the
Rhine, he was livid with rage. But later the friend who had been
put up to buy at the auction smuggled the right-hand gloves over
the Rhine too (what the eye doesn't see the heart doesn't grieve
over), and in Waldangeloch he and the dealer sorted both lots
into pairs again, a left and a right, and they sold them for a very
good price at the fair in Frankfurt. But the dealer had already
made one hundred and forty francs on the sale to the customs
man, and saved the duty. Now, how do the Scriptures put it? 'I
had not known lust, except the law had said, Thou shalt not
covet.'

Alphabetical List of German Titles (with English Translation)

Andreas Hofer

Böser Markt (A Bad Bargain)

Das bequeme Schilderhaus (The Cosy Sentry-Box)

Das Bombardement von Kopenhagen (The Bombardment of Copenhagen)

Das letzte Wort (The Last Word)

Das Mittagessen im Hof (Dinner Outside)

Das schlaue Mädchen (The Cunning Girl)

Das seltsame Rezept (An Odd Prescription)

Das wohlbezahlte Gespenst (Settling Accounts with a Ghost)

Das wohlfeile Mittagessen (The Cheap Meal)

Der Barbierjunge von Segringen (The Barber's Boy at Segringen)

Der betrogene Krämer (A Stallholder is Duped)

Der Commandant und die Jäger in Hersfeld (The Commandant and the Light Infantry in Hersfeld)

Der falsche Edelstein (The Fake Gem)

Der fremde Herr (The Strange Gent)

Der Fremdling in Memel (The Stranger in Memel)

Der fromme Rat (Pious Advice)

Der geduldige Mann (The Patient Husband)

Der geheilte Patient (The Cure)

Der Geizige (The Miser)

Der General-Feldmarschall Suwarow (Field Marshal Suvorov)

Der grosse Sanhedrin zu Paris (The Great Sanhedrin in Paris)

Der grosse Schwimmer (The Champion Swimmer)

Der Handschuhhändler (The Glove Merchant)

Der Heiner und der Brassenheimer Müller (Harry and the Miller from Brassenheim)

Der Husar in Neisse (The Hussar in Neisse)

Der kann Deutsch (He Speaks German!)

Der kluge Richter (The Clever Judge)

Der kluge Sultan (The Clever Sultan)
Der Lehrjunge (The Apprentice Boy)
Der listige Steiermarker (The Cunning Styrian)
Der Maulwurf (The Mole)
Der Rekrut (The Recruit)
Der schlaue Husar (The Artful Hussar)
Der schlaue Mann (The Cunning Husband)
Der schlaue Pilgrim (The Sly Pilgrim)
Der Schneider in Pensa (The Tailor at Penza)
Der silberne Löffel (The Silver Spoon)
Der Star von Segringen (The Starling from Segringen)
Der unschuldig Gehenkte (Innocence is Hanged)
Der vorsichtige Träumer (The Careful Dreamer)
Der Wettermacher (The Weather Man)
Der Zahnarzt (The Dentist)
Des Dieben Antwort (The Thief's Reply)
Des Seilers Antwort (The Ropemaker's Reply)
Die drei Diebe (The Three Thieves)
Die falsche Schätzung (The Mistaken Reckoning)
Die leichteste Todesstrafe (The Lightest Death Sentence)
Die Tabaksdose (The Snuffbox)
Ein gutes Rezept (A Good Prescription)
Ein teurer Kopf und ein wohlfeiler (A Dear Head and a Cheap One)
Ein Wort gibt das andere (One Word Leads to Another)
Eine merkwürdige Abbitte (An Unusual Apology)
Eine sonderbare Wirtszeche (Strange Reckoning at the Inn)
Einträglicher Rätselhandel (A Profitable Game of Riddles)
Etwas aus der Türkei (A Report from Turkey)
Franziska
Gleiches mit Gleichem (Tit for Tat)
Glück und Unglück (Mixed Fortunes)
Gute Antwort (Well Replied)
Gute Geduld (Patience Rewarded)
Gutes Wort, böse Tat (Well Spoken, Badly Behaved)
Heimliche Enthauptung (A Secret Beheading)
Herr Charles (Mr Charles)

Hochzeit auf der Schildwache (Married on Sentry Duty)

Ist der Mensch ein wunderliches Geschöpf (What a Strange Creature is Man)

Kaiser Napoleon und die Obstfrau in Brienne (The Emperor Napoleon and the Fruit Woman in Brienne)

Kannitverstan

Kurze Station (A Short Stage)

List gegen List (Cunning Meets its Match)

Merkwürdige Gespenster-Geschichte (A Curious Ghost Story)

Merkwürdige Schicksale eines jungen Engländers (The Strange Fortunes of a Young Englishman)

Moses Mendelssohn

Rettung einer Offiziersfrau (An Officer's Wife is Saved)

Schlechter Gewinn (A Bad Win)

Schlechter Lohn (A Poor Reward)

Schreckliche Unglücksfälle in der Schweiz (Terrible Disasters in Switzerland)

Seltsame Ehescheidung (A Strange Divorce)

Seltsamer Spazierritt (A Strange Walk and Ride)

Suwarow (Suvorov)

Teure Eier (Expensive Eggs)

Untreue schlägt den eigenen Herrn (Treachery Gets its Just Reward)

Unverhofftes Wiedersehen (Unexpected Reunion)

Wie der Zundelfrieder eines Tages aus dem Zuchthaus entwich und glücklich über die Grenze kam (How One Day Freddy Tinder Escaped from Prison and Came Safely over the Border)

Wie der Zundelfrieder und sein Bruder dem roten Dieter abermal einen Streich spielen (How Freddy Tinder and his Brother Played Another Trick on Carrot-Top Jack)

Wie eine greuliche Geschichte durch einen gemeinen Metzgerhund ist an das Tageslicht gebracht worden (How a Ghastly Story was Brought to Light by a Common or Garden Butcher's Dog)

Wie einmal ein schönes Ross um fünf Prügel feil gewesen ist (How a Fine Horse was Offered for Sale for Five of the Best)

Wie man aus Barmherzigkeit rasiert wird (A Shave as an Act of Charity)

Wie man in den Wald schreit, so schreit es daraus (You get as much as
  you give)
Wie sich der Zundelfrieder hat beritten gemacht (How Freddy Tinder
  Got Himself a Horse to Ride)
Willige Rechtspflege (A Willing Justice)
Zwei Erzählungen (Two Stories)
Zwei honette Kaufleute (Two Honest Tradesmen)

Notes

p. 5 Reference to events in two items ('Mancherlei Regen' and 'Fürchterlicher Kampf eines Menschen mit einem Wolf') in previous issues of the *Hausfreund,* not included in the present volume.

p. 26 The historical events in this paragraph span the years 1755 to 1807 – Lisbon earthquake, 1755; Seven Years War, 1755–63; Francis I of Austria died, 1765; First Partition of Poland, 1772, Second Partition, 1793, Third Partition, 1795; Jesuit Order suppressed by Pope Clement XIV, 1793; Empress Maria Theresa died, 1780; the Danish politician Johan Frederick Struensee executed for treason, 1772; American Declaration of Independence, 1776; siege of Gibraltar, 1779–83; Major (Baron von) Stein commanded a company of Austrian troops who held out for 21 days when surrounded by the Turks at the Veterane Caves near Orsova (a town now in Rumania), 1788; Joseph II died, 1790; Gustavus III of Sweden's campaign against Russia, 1788–90; Leopold II died, 1792; defeat of Prussia by Napoleon, 1806; bombardment of Copenhagen, 1807 (see Note to page 63).

p. 28 By means of the following, largely accurate, report on the Great Sanhedrin summoned by Napoleon, Hebel is saying that the political emancipation of the Jews is only right, but that it must be accompanied by moves towards social integration to be taken by the Jews themselves (perhaps under pressure from the government). When Hebel wrote this piece, new legislation on the constitutional standing of the Jews in his own state of Baden was being prepared.

p. 29 A reference to Napoleon's campaign of 1806–07 against Prussia and Russia.

p. 33 See Note to page 29.

p. 33 Confederation of the Rhine: The confederation of southern and western German states, including Baden, formed in 1806 and allied to Napoleon.

p. 36 The Russo-Turkish War of 1806–12.

p. 37 See Note to page 29. The action of this story took place on 21 February 1807. The 'French' commandant was a German, Colonel Johann Baptist Lingg, serving with the Baden infantry and the troops of the Confederation of the Rhine under Napoleon.

p. 42 Napoleon entered Berlin on 27 October 1806.

p. 43 Napoleon's campaign against Prussia and Russia 1806–07.

p. 44 The Russian Field Marshal Alexander Vasilievich, Count Suvorov (1729–1800), campaigned against Turkey and Poland and against Napoleon in Northern Italy and Switzerland.

p. 55 Moses Mendelssohn (1729–86), friend of the dramatist Gotthold Ephraim Lessing (1729–81) (and the model for his *Nathan the Wise*), was himself an important figure in the German Enlightenment; he worked as a clerk for a Berlin businessman.

p. 56 Stanislaus II, reigned 1764–95. His reforms called forth violent opposition within Poland.

p. 57 A reference to Hebel's source, 'Die drei Diebe', a poem by J. H. Voss (1751–1826).

p. 61 After taking Cairo but losing his fleet at Aboukir, Napoleon marched north and defeated Ottoman forces at Tabor near Nazareth in April 1799.

p. 63 After the Peace of Tilsit (July 1807), Britain feared that Napoleon and the Czar would seize neutral fleets for their own use. The raid on Copenhagen, September 1807, was intended to forestall such a move.

p. 64 Sir William Congreve (1772–1828) – the report of his death in this story is incorrect.

p. 100 Joseph II (1741–90), known for his enlightened policies.

p. 110 The Fifth War of the Coalition against Napoleon, 1809.

p. 118 See Note to page 44. Suvorov was made a Prince in 1799 in recognition of his victories against the French in Italy.

p. 120 In 1809 the Tyroleans under Andreas Hofer rose against Napoleon and Bavaria. Austria had been obliged to cede Tyrol to Bavaria at the Peace of Pressburg 1805.

p. 122 See previous Note. Hofer continued fighting, ignoring cease-fires and the Peace of Schönbrunn (October 1809) in which Austria again renounced its claims to the Tyrol.

p. 126 A battle during the War of Spanish Succession (1701–14) in which Britain, Austria and Holland were in conflict with France.

p. 140 The devout King of Judah whose prayers saved Jerusalem from the Assyrians – see 2 Kings 18–20.

p. 141 The naval battle between British and Dutch fleets, 1781.

p. 142 An incident during Napoleon's campaign in Northern Italy, 1796.

p. 150 France after the declaration of the republic, 22 September 1792.

p. 154 The disastrous crossing of the river Beresina, November 1812, by Napoleon's *grande armée* on the retreat from Moscow; Napoleon abandoned this army before it reached Vilna.

p. 154 The *grand armée* included troops from the Confederation of the Rhine and from Prussia, Saxony and Austria.

p. 162 When Napoleon entered Moscow it had been abandoned and burnt by the retreating Russians (September 1812).